SEEKER'S PROPHECY

SEEKER'S WORLD, BOOK SIX

K. A. RILEY

Copyright © 2023 by K. A. Riley

All rights reserved.

No part of this book may be reproduced in any form or by any electronic or mechanical means, including information storage and retrieval systems, without written permission from the author, except for the use of brief quotations in a book review.

*To everyone who started this journey with Vega and me long ago:
Thank you.*

CONTENTS

1. The Boy — 1
2. The Smith — 5
3. The Rose Wing — 10
4. Assembly — 16
5. Looming War — 21
6. Vision — 25
7. Help — 30
8. Old Friends — 35
9. The Aradia Coven — 40
10. Lachlan — 44
11. Bad Tidings — 51
12. A Plan — 54
13. To the Road — 57
14. Confrontation — 61
15. The Wizard — 68
16. Regrets — 73
17. Relief — 75
18. Prison — 80
19. Home — 84
20. B.F.F. — 88
21. Intruders — 93
22. Farewell to Fairhaven — 99
23. The Mistress — 104
24. A Truce — 111
25. Back to the Rose Wing — 117
26. Destruction — 123
27. Calm Before the Storm — 132
28. Dawn — 139
29. Readying for War — 143
30. Battlefield — 149
31. War — 155
32. It Begins — 160
33. War Wounds — 166

34. Loss	169
35. The Lyre of Adair	174
36. Uldrach	181
37. The Last Battle	187
38. Intervention	191
39. The Sword of Viviane	196
40. The Infirmary	201
41. Coronation	204
42. Plans	210
Epilogue	215
Afterword	219
Coming Soon: Thrall	221
Also by K. A. Riley	225
K. A. Riley on Social Media	231

1
THE BOY

THE BOY COULDN'T HAVE BEEN MORE THAN EIGHT OR NINE years old.

The ancient wooden chair had been crafted for someone far taller than he was, and so his small leather shoes dangled a foot or so off the ground.

He kicked nervously, like his feet were aching to hit the stone tiles and flee.

"What did the queen's soldiers ask you?" Merriwether's voice was as warm and cautious as a tentative hand stroking a frail, frightened kitten.

At first, the boy didn't reply. Instead, his eyes moved around the room, first studying the tall, gray-haired man in front of him, then Callum, who looked as noble and kingly as any young man ever had. His blue eyes shone bright with a combination of curiosity and quiet rage.

He wasn't angry at the innocent boy, of course—but at the people who had forced us all into this situation.

The boy's timid gaze landed on me, zeroing in to study my features as if he knew I was the anomaly in the room.

For a second, I thought I saw a flicker of a smile on his lips—

but whether it was one of nervousness or friendliness, I couldn't entirely tell.

No. Frightened kittens don't smile.

"Go on," I said, trying to emulate my grandfather's calming tone. "It's okay—we're all friends here. We won't hurt you. I promise."

The boy's eyes widened.

He swallowed, then said, "They..."

His voice shook through the lone syllable and his gaze shifted to the floor, his lip quivering.

"It's all right," my grandfather said, and I could feel a jolt of calming magic on the air with each word. "Take your time. No one is putting pressure on you. We're friends, like Vega said. We're here to help."

Searching for reassurance, the boy shot me another look. Instinct told me to take a step toward him. I surrendered to the urge and crouched in front of him, my eyes locked on his.

"Davith," I half-whispered. "That's your name, right?"

He nodded.

"Would you like some chocolate, Davith?"

I wasn't even sure he knew what chocolate was, but his energy shifted as if his fear had been replaced with the sudden realization that he was starving.

With his head cocked to the side, his eyes went wide.

Finally, he nodded vigorously. I let out a quiet laugh, passed one hand over the other, then showed him what I'd summoned.

A perfect cube of milk chocolate filled with sweet strawberry cream.

"Take it," I said. "It's yours."

He hesitated only for a second before reaching for the chocolate, quickly popping it in his mouth.

"There's more where that came from," I told him. "As much as you'd like."

He grabbed my hand, turning it over, trying to work out where the delicious treat had come from.

"Not yet," I said. "Not until you answer the question."

Davith sucked in his lower lip, nodded, then finally said, "They wanted to know if my parents are loyal."

"Loyal? To whom?" Callum asked. I could hear the strain in his voice, and I knew instantly what he was thinking.

This is my sister's doing. The Usurper is up to her usual tricks.

"Loyal to the queen," Davith replied with a half-hearted shrug, confirming what we were all thinking. "They wanted to know if my father would fight against her army. Then…they asked if he and my mother support the Academy for the Blood-Born."

"I see," I said, looking up at Merriwether, then back to the boy. "And what did you tell them?"

"I told them…" he said, his voice shaking once again. "I…"

"It's all right. Keep going. I promise you won't get in trouble." I conjured another chocolate and when Davith had swallowed it, he continued.

"I told them my parents weren't fighters. But the soldiers… they didn't believe me. They said they'd been through my father's things. They saw the Sigil of the Academy on an old piece of fabric in his dresser. That was when they…"

His voice cut off then, and for the first time, I saw the trauma in his eyes. The sorrow of a child who'd lost his parents.

An emotion I knew far too well.

"The soldiers told me they were taking my mother and father. They said they would look after them, and if I helped their cause, they would free them both."

"Help them?" I asked. "How?"

"They wanted me to tell them if there was anyone else in our town who was a traitor."

"And what did you say?"

"I told them I didn't know anything," he said. His lower lip was quivering again, tears rolling down his rosy cheeks. "No one talks about loyalty here. Not to other people. They whisper secrets…but no one talks. It's a happy town. Everyone gets along. No one wants a war. No one…"

"I know, Davith," I said, conjuring another chocolate and handing it to him. "And I know sweets can't make up for your parents' absence. Trust me when I say we will help bring them back if we possibly can. And all the other parents who have been taken."

"Thank you." He took the chocolate from me and squeezed it in his fist. "There was…one other thing they asked."

"Oh?" I threw Merriwether a quick look before pulling my eyes back to the boy and giving him a reassuring smile. "What is it?"

"They said they're looking for a…a blacksmith, I think."

"A blacksmith?" I repeated. "Why?"

Davith shook his head. "They didn't say. All they told me was that he was special. They said he's dressed in silver and that he has eyes of gold. That he shines like the sun."

"Thank you, Davith," Merriwether said abruptly, stepping forward and laying a hand on my shoulder as if to tell me it was time to stop the questioning. "That will be all. You've been very helpful. I'm afraid it's time for us to leave now."

Silently, I turned to follow my grandfather and Callum out of the small house. But first, I flicked a hand toward the rickety-looking table under the nearest window, conjuring six boxes of cream-filled chocolates.

The boy deserved so much more.

I only wished I could give it to him.

2
THE SMITH

"What will happen to him?" I asked when the three of us had made our way outside and left Davith under the watchful eye of two Rangers.

"He'll be looked after by his aunt, who lives in a cottage not far from here," Merriwether said. "When he's older, if he chooses, he can come and train with us at the Academy to be anything he likes. I suspect your chocolates have already been enough to gain his loyalty for life."

"I wish I could give him his parents instead," I said bitterly.

"His father was a former student of ours," Merriwether said. "A Ranger. Unfortunate that the enemy uncovered the evidence of our affiliation."

"It's the same story everywhere in these lands," Callum added with a grimace. "Adults disappearing in every town, all because they're under suspicion. It's nothing more than a Witch Hunt."

"If only they were hunting *actual* Witches," I said, "there would be consequences for their cruelty. But these are innocent humans who are being taken away. The queen is culling the Otherwhere, getting rid of anyone who doesn't support her body, mind, and soul. Which means there won't be much of the Otherwhere's population left soon, other than those who recognize her as the rightful queen." I turned to look toward the small house's front door. "I don't even know if Davith's parents are still alive. Maybe we should look for—"

"You *do* know," Merriwether interrupted, his voice deep and quiet. "As do we all."

When I looked into his eyes, I could see reality reflecting back at me. A sickening, horrible truth.

The Usurper Queen was creating a land filled with orphans, and she couldn't have cared less. She wanted the realm populated by tortured souls unable to fend for themselves, so they would one day have little choice but to declare their loyalty to her—the very leader who had taken their parents from them.

Just as she took mine long ago.

It's easier to reign over those who are helpless than those who are strong.

"Why would they be looking for a blacksmith?" I asked, trying to take my mind off the queen's cruelty. "Is the enemy's army short on weapons or something?"

"Not exactly." Merriwether's brow creased, and I could see a new, menacing worry in his eyes. "The man they're searching for is no common smith. The queen is not on the hunt for weaponry. I'm afraid she's searching for something far more nefarious—something permanent."

"What do you mean?" Callum asked, looking as confused as I was.

"There is a man...or rather, a *being*, known as the Lightsmith. He moves about the lands quietly, skulking like a shadow. He's a creature of mischief. He has no alliances, and he possesses powers that are a threat to us all. The queen is seeking him out because she failed to obtain any of the four Relics of Power. She fears she will not be strong enough to defeat us without them."

"So this Lightsmith is planning to steal the Relics?" I asked. "Is that even possible?"

"That isn't his intention," Merriwether replied. "The Lightsmith is not exactly a thief. He is a creature of High Magic, and his sole purpose for existing is to destroy."

"You mean," Callum said softly, "he could *break* the Relics?"

"He could, if he were persuaded to do so—whether by someone else or by his own depraved mind." Merriwether sighed. He began to walk, and Callum and I flanked him, keeping up with his long strides. "The four Relics—the Sword, the Scepter, the Lyre, the Orb—each of them represents a strength. The Sword of Viviane, the weapon that once belonged to King Arthur, is pure brawn. It contains within its steel the power to take down the strongest beings, so long as it's wielded by the right fighter. The Lyre represents the mind—control, intellect, strategy, peace, and even war. It can be used to influence massive numbers of enemies, if one knows how to use it properly. The Orb of Kilarin grants the gift of Sight, and it gives its keepers the ability to see through time and space. The Scepter of Morgana is a Relic that can only be wielded by a creature of High Magic," Merriwether added. "You, Vega, have used it. You know its power."

"I used it in the Melding," I replied with a nod. "To bring Callum and Caffall back together after the Severing."

It was a bittersweet memory—both awful and wonderful. With the Scepter of Morgana, I had cast the spell that had saved Callum's life and that had reunited him with his dragon Caffall, strengthening them both so that they could exist separate from one another.

I didn't like thinking about that moment, about the pain that had come with watching Callum suffer. But now, seeing him strong, his bond with Caffall unbreakable, it finally seemed almost worth the torment we'd been through.

"The Scepter can be used for the greatest good," Merriwether said. "The queen knows she lacks the power to wield it, so she wants it gone—along with the other Relics. She wants them destroyed once and for all, never to return. She knows that if the four objects remain in our possession for the near future, she doesn't stand a chance against us in the final battle for the throne."

"I wonder why she gave up on them so easily when the Seekers were looking for them, then," I said. "The Scepter—the Orb—she didn't send anyone to find them."

"She had no Seekers left who were willing to help her. Not to mention that somewhere along the way, she remembered that the Lightsmith exists. She knows that destroying the Relics would be a more effective strategy at this point than trying to find them. So, under the guise of her hunt for traitors, she's searching for the smith. Her soldiers are making their way from town to town in their search, killing as they go and leaving ruin in their wake."

"Are we sure this Lightsmith even exists?" Callum asked. "Has anyone ever encountered him?"

Merriwether nodded solemnly, stopping in the middle of the cobbled, dirty street recently trampled by dozens of Waergs' paws and soldiers' boots. "I had an altercation with him years ago, and it was…unpleasant," he said. "His power is frightening, even to me. It's been a long time, but I can feel him on the air once again, now that the Relics have revealed themselves. There is no doubt in my mind that Lumus feels his presence, as well. I suspect it was his idea to begin the hunt."

"*Lumus*," I repeated, my voice tinged with hatred.

The silver-eyed husband of the Usurper Queen was an evil, calculating warlock bent on ensuring that his wife maintain her place on the throne. "Of *course* he's the one sending Waergs out to kill innocent people. He's the only person I can think of who's even crueler than the queen."

"He will stop at nothing to keep Callum—or anyone else—from taking the throne from his dear wife," Merriwether said. "He's loyal to a fault. If the castle Uldrach falls and the city of Kaer Uther crumbles to dust at last, then he and the queen, too, will fall. The kingdom will be renewed and those two will be driven from the land, along with their pest of a son. We have enemies all over the Otherwhere, but Lumus is the most powerful and desperate of them. We must not underestimate his power…or the strength of his desire."

"The Relics," I said. "They're safely hidden, aren't they?"

"As safe as they can be," Merriwether replied. "Three of them —the Scepter, the Sword, and the Lyre—are in the Academy's vaults. The Orb is concealed elsewhere, though if you should ever need it, Vega, you know how to find it."

"I do?" I asked, feeling suddenly flustered. Was I supposed to have some power no one had ever told me about?

Merriwether simply smiled and gave me a quick nod. "Of course. But come, let's head back to the Academy. We have warnings to dole out to the students, and I will do so in the morning. I'm afraid that tonight will be the last chance we have to relax for some time."

3
THE ROSE WING

AFTER DINNER THAT EVENING, CALLUM AND I SAT IN THE LIVING room in the Academy's Rose Wing.

Large and bright with luxurious furnishings, our suite was the most peaceful, relaxing place I'd ever had the pleasure of inhabiting.

That night, though, the air was filled with tension.

Every time I told myself not to worry, I found myself growing more fearful. Cushions and soft blankets that should have felt cozy and comfortable suddenly seemed hard and angular. The fire dancing in the hearth looked menacing, rather than warm and inviting.

A veil of silence had fallen over the space around us. Not because Callum and I had nothing to say to one another — if anything, there was too *much* to say.

I knew without asking that Callum was deep in thought. He had always had the air of a formidable ruler, and he was now pondering the dangerous days ahead, wondering how he and Caffall could spread themselves thin and wide enough to combat every small force the queen sent out to the Otherwhere's various corners.

"Gold coin for your thoughts?" I finally said with a crooked smile.

Worried though I was, I wanted to lighten his mood, to diminish his mental load.

I wanted to help.

"I was just thinking there's only one Caffall," he said simply. "Only one golden dragon. As strong as he is, he can only be in one place at a time. The queen is showing us that she intends to split our focus by attacking multiple sites at once. Her forces are moving in smaller groups than I'd imagined, taking down many towns at the same time."

"One Caffall is a hell of a lot better than none," I said.

Callum rose to his feet, dragged a hand through his hair, and sighed. "My sister's tactic is to pull our eyes from one end of the Otherwhere to the other and back again. To distract us, to spread our forces so thin that we have no real strength in any one location. She wants to weaken us slowly, methodically. Rather than one huge battle, she's begun inflicting death by a thousand cuts. She's angry that we have the Relics. Angry that we have fierce allies. It's why she's questioning the loyalty of everyone in the entire realm. She wants to make the citizens fearful, to teach them that helping our side equals death. She wants to terrorize and paralyze them. It turns them against each other, makes them paranoid."

"So we'll have to find a way to fight her tactics," I said. "We need to talk to the people. Show them that we're on their side. We need to protect them."

"How, Vega?" Callum said, turning and laying a hand on the mantle, staring into the fire. "How can we protect them from what she's doing? There are only so many of us—and as strong as you and I are—as strong as Merriwether is—I just don't know if it's possible."

I'd rarely seen Callum looking helpless or at his wit's end, and it was disconcerting, to say the least.

"I'm supposedly meant to become king," he said miserably. "But right now, I'm doubting my worthiness. I need more hands, more eyes. More strength. Instead of one army, I need several. And I'm coming to the realization far too late."

"That's because you're putting all the pressure on yourself," I said. "No one can protect an entire realm, whether they think they can or not. Besides, it's *not* too late. We haven't lost yet."

"It's the king's job," he said. "I only wish I could ride out tonight and take on Isla's forces myself, to fight for my people. I feel like my hands are tied. I may not be king yet, but I'm meant to protect."

"No, that's the job of those you put in charge of leading the fight," I said, rising to my feet as he scowled at the dancing flames. I stepped toward him and put my arms around his waist, pressing my cheek to his back. "You need to learn to call on others when it's too much. You have many allies outside the Academy, remember."

He went silent for a moment before saying, "You're right." He turned to me, pulling my hands from his waist and kissing them. "Tomorrow morning after the Assembly, I'll fly up to meet with Kohrin Icewalker and some other leaders. We'll spread out and cover as much territory as we can. We need to stop the queen's smaller forces before she does any more damage."

"Good." I smiled to think of Kohrin, the Grell I'd met in my early days in the Otherwhere. He was strong, loyal, and a valuable ally to the Academy and all who opposed the queen.

I pushed myself up onto my toes and kissed Callum. "Come, sit with me. Let's talk about something else. Let's pretend we're not on the brink of war…just for a minute."

I managed to persuade him over to the couch, where we plopped down, me leaning against his chest, his arms around me.

"What should we talk about, Miss Sloane?" he asked.

"Well…" I began, my courage suddenly gone. "I was thinking…"

"Yes?"

"It's July. In a few days, I'll be eighteen." I sighed. "Even though time passes differently here in the Otherwhere—and even though it feels like fifty years since I turned *seventeen*."

"I know it does." I could feel the smile in Callum's entire body, his arms tightening around me. "Speaking of your coming birthday, you know I don't intend to pressure you, but…"

"Don't you?" Laughing, I pulled away and looked up into his blue eyes, the shade of an arctic lake. So deep, so filled with a mystery that had always lured me in. All the experience and knowledge of a person who'd lived over a century with all the sweetness and innocence of someone as young as I was.

I pulled my eyes once again to the ring on my left hand. It was flickering now with the reflection of the nearby fire, alive with an internal flame that half frightened and half thrilled me.

The ring felt in that moment like a symbol of our entire relationship. One filled with unknowns, with power, with raging flame that felt like it could both create and destroy.

"Are you worried that it's still too soon?" Callum asked. "Too soon to commit to a future here, I mean?"

I couldn't imagine ever wanting anything or anyone else. Callum was the love of my life, and though I knew my feelings for him might grow and evolve, I also knew they weren't in any danger of fading.

On top of that, I couldn't imagine saying goodbye to the Otherwhere…or to the second version of myself I'd discovered in this place.

I shook my head. "I feel like I've lived two lifetimes since we met. I know I'm young, but I don't feel like it anymore. Sometimes I think my parents would have had a fit to hear me talking about commitment at the age of eighteen." I took in a deep breath before adding, "But I also think they would have understood."

Callum's brows raised. "Do you?"

I nodded. "My mother would have loved you. My father

would have, too, although he would never have said it in so many words. He wasn't the most expressive guy in the world. He definitely kept his cards very close to his chest."

At that, Callum smiled. "Tell me about them," he said. "Tell me what it was like to grow up with them."

"It was…amazing," I said. Reaching into my mind for the memories I seldom touched for fear of the pain they might inflict, I smiled. "One time, when Will and I were little, our family took a trip to the Atlantic coast—to Cape Cod. Will and I thought we'd go swimming in the ocean. We were so excited about it. But when we got there, I discovered how cold the water was. I took one step into it and shrieked. Will was a little braver, but I could tell that even he wasn't about to dive in head-first. So my father scooped us both up, put us in the car, and took us for ice cream. We sat at a picnic table and looked out over the ocean, and my mother told me, 'You're not a child of water, Vega. The ocean's cold isn't in your blood. You have a warm heart because you are a child of fire—a magical being.'" I turned to look at the flames licking at the blackened stone lining the fireplace. "I don't know how she knew back then. My mother wasn't the one with magical blood—yet she knew what I would become."

"Or maybe she was more magical than you ever thought," Callum said. "There are more things in heaven and earth, Horatio, than are dreamt of in your philosophy…'"

"Hamlet?" I laughed. "I always forget you know so much about my world." The first time I'd met Callum, he had impressed me with his knowledge of books—of course, at that time, I hadn't even known he was from another world entirely.

"I'm just saying there is magic in many of us…magic we don't even know about. Some see beyond their narrow line of vision. Others have a sense about people…something deep and instinctive and powerful. We may not *call* it magic, but it's greater than simple human thoughts and feelings."

"Well, well. You're being very deep this evening, Lord Drake."

"I still want to know what makes you tick," he said with a grin. "Even after all this time, I'm still trying to learn about the deepest parts of you. I realize I can never meet your parents, but through your memories and mind, I can, perhaps, get to know them just a little."

To my surprise and delight, we spoke about them for two more hours at least, with Callum plying me with questions about their work, their favorite places, the bedtime stories they read us when we were small…

After a while, I grew convinced that my memories were fueling Callum as much as me. His childhood had been brief and fraught with pain. His parents, who should have loved and nurtured him, had treated him with a coldness and a loathing that was beyond cruel.

No child should ever have to feel so reviled by their own parents.

If it took me the rest of my life to prove to Callum how worthy of love he was, then I would make sure he knew.

He was the best person I had ever met. He was noble, kind, fair-minded and uncompromising in his loyalty. He would throw himself in front of an Ursal to protect me or anyone else he loved —and for that alone, he was deserving of affection.

Sharing stories from my past with him seemed to cleanse us both. But it also reminded each of us that there was good in the world.

In the days ahead, we were going to need all the good we could find.

4
ASSEMBLY

The following morning after breakfast, Callum kissed me gently before an intent gaze and a raised brow reminded me we had an Assembly to attend.

"I'm not looking forward to this," I told him as we strode down the corridor toward the stone staircase.

"Neither am I," Callum said. "But we both know it must be done."

The mood in the Academy's Great Hall was somber and electric at once.

Not that I was surprised. The entire Academy for the Blood-Born had felt like this for days, ever since I'd returned to the Otherwhere after the conclusion of my final year of high school.

Every student knew the war had begun, and that the time to risk their lives for the realm was finally at hand.

Any normal human would have been terrified at the prospect. But the Zerkers, Casters, and Rangers of the Academy were all aware—and delighted—that everything they'd learned was about to be put to the test.

While some of us just wanted to go home and curl up on the couch with a comforting book, the air in the Great Hall sizzled with the thrill of those who had spent the last few years of their lives itching to go to war and prove their mettle.

The Great Hall's seats were filling rapidly with the school's color-coded denizens in their red, blue, and green tunics. All of them were now official graduates of an institution that had taught them to fight and to win.

Restless and itching for battle, they waited breathlessly for Merriwether's coming announcement.

The Academy was closed for business—at least for now. There would be no more classes and no more official training so long as the Otherwhere was preparing for full-blown war. No more official tests or competitions. Every bit of instruction from here on out was intended to help our side defend against an impossibly strong enemy on the battlefield.

The Usurper Queen had an army of Waergs—humans with the ability to shift into massive wolves. But the even more daunting fighters were the Ursals, the enormous bears trained to take down anyone and everyone in their path—including, at times, their own forces.

The Zerkers, the rebellious warriors of the Academy who normally sat at the back of the Great Hall, were seated in the front rows. For once, they looked disciplined and attentive, their eyes locked onto Merriwether, who made his way onto the dais as Callum and I watched from the back of the large chamber.

When the Zerkers turned to whisper to one another, I could practically see the drool dripping from the corners of their mouths. They couldn't wait to fight, desperate as they were to put all their training to good use. And I, for one, was grateful that they were so keen to risk their lives.

I was also baffled.

"I'll never understand how anyone can be happy about a war," I said under my breath.

"They're each convinced they'll be heroes, which sounds ridiculous, I know," Callum replied, "but it's the only way they'll get through this without losing their minds." He pressed close enough to me that our upper arms were touching—a sensation that set off a wave of butterflies in my stomach.

Still, after all this time and so many nights spent entangled in one another's arms, it excited me to be near him.

"For months on end," he added, "we've trained them to fight. They've learned about the Usurper Queen's treachery and Lumus' power. They're filled with anger—*and* they know they're on the right side of this war, which gives them all the more motivation to win."

I looked up at him, studying his eyes as I asked, "Do you really think our numbers are enough to defeat the queen's army? There are so few of us, and the Ursals are huge. It would take ten Zerkers to take down one of them."

Callum leaned in closer when he said, "If all we had were those of us in this room, I would agree. But don't forget—the Academy has been training fighters for many years, and those fighters live in every region of the Otherwhere. The lands are full of Rangers, Zerkers, Casters. They'll help us."

He ground his jaw for a moment then added almost absently, "Still, I don't think this war will be won on the field of battle."

Puzzled, I furrowed my brow. "Where, then?"

"Uldrach, my sister's stolen castle. If we don't stop Isla—the Usurper Queen, I mean—and Lumus, we don't stand a chance. And trust me when I say my darling sister won't be running into battle with a shield in hand and armor on. She's too cowardly to be a warrior. Which means we'll have to play her sordid games in her own domain."

I crossed my arms over my chest and nodded, staring out at the large chamber and recalling a time long ago—yet *not* so long ago—when I'd stood in this very place with my friend Niala and her shape-shifting familiar, Rourke. Niala was currently studying spellcasting with the Witches in the Aradia Coven. She was my closest friend at the Academy and was fiercely loyal to the cause.

During those early days in this magical realm, I had been absolutely terrified of drawing attention to myself. All I'd wanted was to sink into the floor and disappear from everyone's view for eternity.

Now, I looked over the crowd with the quiet confidence of someone who had been through her share of battles, pain, and torment.

More than once, I'd stared death in the face and somehow come through it in one piece. I'd watched friends die. I'd watched Callum come far too close to death, himself.

I was no longer innocent. No longer the frightened teenage girl I'd once been, convinced I would fail at every possible test that was thrown my way. I would soon fall, metaphorical and literal weapons drawn, into adulthood. I would have choices to make—difficult ones—and a future to plan.

But only if I survived the war now raging all over the Otherwhere.

Dread filled me as I realized how much death and destruction I was likely to witness in the coming days.

I still had weaknesses. Yet, I had grown stronger than I'd ever imagined I could be. I was a Seeker. A Summoner. There were some who now called me *Sorcière*, a fancy word for a High Witch —and I wore the title with all the pride in the world.

I felt powerful, if not entirely confident in my place in this land...or even in my own world.

My mind racing, I glanced down at my left hand, my eyes landing on the beautiful ring Callum had given me months ago. It was a sort of promise ring—though he hadn't pressured me to commit the rest of my life to him, and I had made no promises. We had agreed that it was more symbolic than binding, a reminder of what we'd endured together and what our bond meant to us both.

The three red stones reflected the flickering flame-light of the sconces and torches that floated along the Great Hall's walls. The center stone had once been part of the dragon key that had first allowed me to escape my world and come to this one. It was an amplifier stone—one filled with powerful magic.

As my eyes fixed on the shimmering stones, my heart surged with fear and affection all rolled up into one heart-wrenching emotion.

I wasn't yet sure what role I'd have to play in the coming battle. But I knew, at least, that I was loved by the most extraordinary person I'd ever met.

It was a beautiful thought—one that was interrupted by a sudden shudder of horror.

As if rebelling against my brief burst of joy, my mind twisted and turned, filling with a river of memories I didn't entirely want to revisit.

Someone *else* had loved me, too—or at least, he'd *thought* he did.

When I had fought Lachlan at the castle on the coast where Callum had confronted Meligant, I'd summoned five Fire Spirits armed with flaming bows and arrows.

At my command and in a moment of desperation, they had shot Lachlan before vanishing again.

The creatures I'd drawn to me had taken down one of my best friends, powerful though he was. With a simple manipulation of my mind, I had called for aid, and it had come to me.

It was a gift I'd never asked for—an ability to conjure entities I hadn't even known existed.

But at what cost?

I made a mental note to find Lachlan and check in on him, to make sure he was healing...and to ask his forgiveness once again.

For now, though, I pulled my eyes to my grandfather who stood statue-still before the small army of warriors he'd helped train.

5
LOOMING WAR

The Headmaster—otherwise known as my grandfather—cleared his throat as he looked over the crowd.

I took hold of Callum's hand, squeezing it as Merriwether raised his arms to quiet the audience's excited murmurs.

"My friends," he called out, his voice booming through the space like a force of nature. "Full-blown war has come to our lands. Your forebears—those who trained here at the Academy over many years—are out in the field, fighting to defend the Otherwhere's citizens and their homes. Thousands of our allies are scattered through this land, doing all they can to push the Usurper Queen's forces back. Some of you…" he added, looking down at the rows of overzealous Zerkers, "…are excited and eager to do battle. But I warn you now—this will not be the simple target practice to which you are accustomed. It's no game. The queen has recruited warriors who fight at a level far beyond yours. Her army is a brutal, soulless force, bent solely on killing humans who wear the Academy's sigil—and determined to take down our allies, be they Witches, Grells, or anyone else."

A buzz of voices rose up in the crowd. I heard the word "Ursal" thrown around once or twice, panic swelling at the mention of the massive bears under the Usurper Queen's command.

I leaned in close to Callum again and said, "I've never understood why we didn't attack the queen before the Ursals were trained. Wouldn't it have given us the best chance? We could have taken them by surprise and stopped the war before it had a chance to start."

He winced. "Our best hope is to strike when Uldrach is mostly empty and the army is doing battle on the fields of the Otherwhere. That will be the time when the queen and Lumus are at their most vulnerable."

When I looked doubtful, Callum added, "Try not to worry. Merriwether has a plan, as always."

"What plan could possibly succeed at this point?"

He lowered his chin then and smiled, and I knew exactly what he was thinking. "You know Merriwether. He never explains his thought process. He only tells me the minimum. Still, I trust him with my life. Have faith in your grandfather, Vega. He will do everything in his power to keep us alive."

"The Ursals," Merriwether bellowed from the dais as if reading our minds, "are feral creatures, trained to follow their most predatory instincts—which means killing anything that smells like the enemy. They are one of the few creatures in the Otherwhere who kill humans for sport as well as for sustenance. Combined with the queen's Waergs, they will be an almost unstoppable force—but stop them we must, and there is only one way to do so permanently."

Once again, murmurs rose up in the crowd as the Academy's alumni pondered what he could mean.

"We must take the queen's power from her," Merriwether said. "If we have to demolish her forces to get to her, then that's what we'll do."

In that moment, my grandfather's eyes met mine and his voice entered my mind as Caffall's so often did.

To succeed, we will need strength and brawn—but we need you, as well. You, Vega, are the key to all of this—you and him.

Him, I thought, staring back, searching his face for hidden meaning. *Callum? Lachlan?*

You already know who I'm talking about, he replied.

His words filled me with dread.

Merriwether didn't mention the Lightsmith to the gathered Academy students. It seemed he wanted to keep the destructive creature who was lurking somewhere in the Otherwhere a secret —at least, for now.

If the Usurper Queen really was using him to get hold of the Relics of Power, then everything we Seekers had fought for would be wasted. There would be no stopping her if she successfully destroyed the one advantage we had.

I gritted my teeth as Merriwether spoke. I couldn't let it happen. Couldn't allow all our sacrifice—Callum's near-death Severing from Caffall, Lachlan's pain and torment, our loss of Cairn, a fellow Seeker—to be in vain.

With my breath trapped in my chest, I pulled away and strode quickly out of the room, gasping for air. Seconds later, I was joined in the wide corridor by Callum, who took my hands in his and held on while I inhaled a deep breath and tried to calm my raging heart.

"You're afraid," he said softly. "Was it the mention of the Ursals?"

"No," I said, gasping out a breath. "Though I'm not particularly excited about them. It's just—every time we make some progress, something comes along to trample it. We *found* all the Relics, Callum. We have them in our possession. There was some part of me that hoped it would be enough to stop your sister from going to war—that she would be afraid of our power. But now, Merriwether's in there talking strategy with a room full of wide-eyed teenagers when the truth is, the queen might end us—

especially if the Lightsmith does her bidding and destroys the Relics."

"Don't lose hope, Vega. Yes, the Relics are important, and they've helped us gain strength. But even if they were shattered to pieces, we'd still have Caffall and you, the Witches, the Grells —and others, too."

"I suppose you're right," I said wearily as he put his arms around me and pulled me close. "At least, I hope you are."

As reassuring as his touch was, I felt the weight of a thousand worlds settle on us both. We weren't simply fighting for Callum's seat on the throne—for the true heir to find his rightful place in the Otherwhere.

We were fighting to keep countless people's lives from ending, both in the Otherwhere and at home in Fairhaven. Because if the Usurper Queen won here, I had little doubt she would bring her war to my world.

She would enjoy nothing more than to destroy the home and the town I loved.

And I would sooner die than let that happen.

6

VISION

"I'll be back tonight," Callum said when the students had filed out of the Great Hall, practically bouncing off the stone walls as they went. "Just now, I have a date with a certain dragon."

The words drew a laugh from me, and for that, I was grateful.

Callum cocked his head. "Are you intending to stay at the Academy today?"

I was about to say yes, but something told me it would be a little white lie. I had no specific plans—not yet—but an invisible force seemed to be calling to me from somewhere far away.

"I don't know, honestly," I told him. "I'll go talk to my grandfather, then figure it out. I may venture out for a little."

"You do remember there's a war raging out there, don't you?" Callum asked, jutting his chin toward the windows and beyond.

"Unfortunately, you don't need to remind me. I promise—I'll see you tonight, whatever happens."

He kissed my forehead gently, sighed, then said, "You stay safe, all right?"

Smiling, I replied, "I will if you do the same."

"I have a monstrous beast to watch over me. I'll be okay."

When he had taken off in search of Caffall, I headed to my grandfather's office. For once I walked instead of transporting myself there instantly. I couldn't quite bring myself to rush toward whatever grim fate awaited me.

As I raised my hand to knock on the door, he called out to me to come in.

I snickered.

He never failed to sense when I was close, no matter how silent I might be in my approach.

Merriwether had once told me it was because magic users had an energy to them, an aura that announced their proximity. It made me wonder if Lumus, too, had the power to know if I was near. If he would read me on the air like a scent wafting toward him.

Not that I had any intention of going near the queen's awful husband anytime soon. In fact, I would have happily avoided the warlock like the plague for the rest of my life. But I'd always known, deep in my heart, that the day would come when I'd find myself face to face with him again.

I didn't hate many people, but there was no question that I despised Lumus and his awful wife.

I'd been so naive the first time I'd confronted the queen. There was so much that I hadn't understood about myself, about magic or about the Otherwhere.

But next time, I would be ready.

I pushed Merriwether's door open and stepped inside the warm space filled with books, trinkets, and magical items.

"Come in," he said. "Sit. I was just thinking about you."

"Any particular reason?" I asked, taking a seat opposite him.

"Yes. I'd like to show you something."

But he didn't move, didn't open a drawer. Nothing.

I raised my eyebrows inquisitively. "What is it?"

"The Orb of Kilarin," he said.

"I've seen it. More than once." For a moment, I wondered if his memory was slipping away from him.

"I know," he replied with a chuckle. "I need to know that you can access it."

"I told you, I don't know where it is. I thought you had it hidden somewhere here at the Academy."

"I won't say out loud where it is. The Orb is our most powerful tool against the enemy, and if it should fall into their hands…well, I don't need to tell you what could happen. There's a reason I'm keeping it separate from the other Relics."

He was right. He didn't need to tell me what could happen.

I'd seen it with my own eyes when Lachlan, under his father's influence, had used it to peer into my past—to see my weaknesses, my pain. He had tried to persuade me to erase much of my life in order to move back through time and reunite with my parents.

During the process, he had seen too much of my pain—too much of the sorrow that had haunted my brother Will and me for so long.

The Orb's power was greater than anything I'd ever encountered.

I thought I detected a shudder from my grandfather, but I may simply have imagined it. It wasn't like Merriwether to feel fear, let alone to show it.

Perhaps he was simply sympathizing with my own pain at the recollection.

"You want me to *summon* the Orb," I said quietly, understanding at last.

He nodded. "It's the one Relic I intend to keep separate from the others. The Lightsmith must not have the opportunity to destroy it, whatever occurs. Summon the Orb now, and when we are done with it, it will return to its hiding spot."

I closed my eyes and called to the Relic. I'd seen it enough times that I could picture it easily in my mind's eye: a swirling sphere of purple, glistening and writhing strangely in the light.

My hands reached out, hovering over Merriwether's desk, and at the tips of my fingers, I felt a sort of crackling as if small, tidy electrical shocks were making their way just under my skin.

Gasping with the power surging through me, I opened my eyes to see the Orb floating in mid-air under my hands. It twisted and turned, defying gravity as dark purple smoke morphed in its depths into various shapes.

"What did you want to show me?" I asked Merriwether, my hands trembling.

"Ask the Orb about the Ursals," he said.

"Shouldn't I ask it about the Lightsmith? Can it tell us where he is?"

"Unfortunately, no. His power forbids objects such as the Orb being used to track him." He looked apologetic when he said again, "Go on. Ask it about the Ursals."

I wanted to ask why but instead, I simply looked into the sphere and silently formulated a thought.

What are the Ursals doing? Where has the queen sent them?

The smoke parted to reveal a scene of massive, tank-like bears loping across a clearing toward a small village.

I'd seen the creatures before from Caffall's back as they tore across the landscape. But I had never seen them in full-on attack mode, trampling their way through the countryside on their way to wreak havoc.

The scene horrified me.

"Would they?" I asked myself. "No…they wouldn't."

Surely the bears would stop when they reached the walls of the village, I thought. But as I watched, they crashed effortlessly through the barriers, tearing them down with little more than a few swipes of their front paws and the gnashing of massive fangs.

Screams of horror lashed through the air as men, women, and

children fled through the streets. The Ursals ran them down, stealing away their lives as if the humans were delicate, fluttering moths taken down by a lion's paw.

I cried out, swept my hands over the Orb, and shut my eyes.

"No more," I whimpered. "Please. No more."

7
HELP

A few seconds passed before Merriwether said, "You can open your eyes now. The image is gone."

"Was that real?" I asked, wincing as I looked into the Orb, which once again filled with smoke.

"That depends on what question you posed."

"I asked what the Ursals were doing now."

"Ah." Merriwether reached his hands out and took the Orb, cradling it to his chest. "The bears are simple creatures. They are one of the few natural predators of humans in this land. They were never meant to exist in the same region as humans—never meant to serve us, just as dragons were never meant to be held captive by our species. Yet the queen realized along the way that they would offer her more power—albeit chaotic power—than the Relics. The Ursals sow fear, and fear is the greatest weapon of any tyrant."

So, the Orb had shown me the truth.

The Ursals were currently in the process of killing innocent humans.

"Could the other Relics help us to fight them?" I asked. "Can they possibly be enough against such a destructive force?"

"They could help, yes." Merriwether looked worried. "But only if we are able to wield them when the time comes."

"Why wouldn't we be able to? They're ours."

"It's not quite so simple," he replied. "For instance, the Sword of Viviane can be wielded by only one person until it's passed onto the next."

Uncertain of what he meant, I stared at him for a moment before a sort of clarity came to me.

"The sword once belonged to King Arthur," I said slowly.

"Yes. It's known as Excalibur in your world," Merriwether replied with a nod.

"So you're saying it still belongs to its original wielder?"

"Possibly. Though I have long thought the Sword of Viviane would one day find its way to another. It is my belief that it's more important than the other Relics of Power—but I'm not entirely convinced. Not yet."

"And the Lyre?"

"The Lyre may come into play when the time is right," Merriwether said. "The Lyre controls minds. It creates clarity. At times, it opens doors to other realms. But most importantly, the Lyre can be used to summon."

"Summon?"

My grandfather nodded. "Some say it can call forth a great army—one that hasn't been seen in this land in centuries."

"Why don't we use it right now, then? If we could defeat the queen's army—"

"Because its player is in another land entirely. Never in all its years has the Lyre been used to its full potential. But an old legend tells that when war storms its way through the Otherwhere and the sun turns to blood, the Player shall arrive and strum the tune that will wake the mightiest force this land has ever known."

I had already asked a hundred questions. I felt like a small child, still not satisfied with the information I'd been given. Even so, I asked another one.

"What force? Who are you talking about?"

Merriwether issued a half-smile and said, "Even I am not sure of that, Granddaughter. I suppose we may find out soon enough. But it's quite possible we'll never learn the Lyre's true value."

"Great. We have all kinds of advantages, but we might not be able to use them. But shouldn't Callum have the sword?" I asked. "If there's a chance it's meant for the king..."

"The Sword will find its wielder when the time is right," Merriwether replied, and this time his tone was curt, as if he'd grown weary of my incessant questions. "But it is his or hers to claim—not ours to force on anyone. Besides, a sword won't do Callum much good from his place on Caffall's back."

I let out a sigh. I wanted Callum armed. I wanted to know that no matter what, he would be safe from harm during the battles to come.

But I reminded myself that I couldn't control his fate. I couldn't control *him*.

The only thing I could control was my own actions.

"What can I do?" I asked. "How can I help?"

"Help?" Merriwether asked with a crooked smile. "You have done so much already, Granddaughter. You've brought us the Relics—you and the other Seekers, whom you named to work by your side. You saved Callum's life, and probably Lachlan's, as well. What more do you really want?"

"I want to see Callum on the throne," I said. "I want to see the Usurper Queen overthrown. I want to see Lachlan happy. I want..."

"You want everything," Merriwether replied. "You want the world."

"Is it really so much to ask?" I replied with a snicker.

He laughed. "There are a few things I've wanted for years," he said, his tone wistful. "*Many* years now. Things I could, I suppose, have acquired—a certain simple joy in life, for instance. But it would have meant endangering others and shirking my personal duty. Sometimes, we simply have to focus on what we have to offer, rather than what we feel the universe owes us."

"I don't feel the universe owes me anything," I protested. "I just want the Otherwhere to return to what it once was."

"In the days before the Usurper Queen, you mean."

I nodded. "I want the people to be safe. Happy. I want them to look forward to the future."

"And you? Are you looking forward to the future?" With that, Merriwether held out the Orb, and I found myself looking into it once again. He lowered his hands and the sphere remained in mid-air, floating, defying gravity as it turned slowly.

In it, I saw my own face, a smile on my lips as I pushed my hair behind my ear. A sea of grass and flowers lay behind me.

I turned to see someone running toward me—just a shadow of a person. It wasn't Callum, yet I knew it was someone I cared about deeply.

Whoever it was, I ached to have them near me. I held my arms out…and then they were gone.

"Who was that?" I asked out loud.

"That's for the future to tell you. But the future is not carved in stone. It is what we make it."

"I have no future if Callum doesn't succeed. No future if he…" I stopped, fearful that the words would crumble to dust.

"You know as well as I do that's not true," Merriwether said. "Even if Callum fails—even if he *falls*—you have a future, Vega. In this world or your own."

A tear slipped down my cheek. I wiped it away, angry that my grandfather could even think such a future was possible.

"He can't fail," I said. "He can't fall. He's my life now."

"Well, Vega dear, if there's anyone in the world who will do everything to see to it that he succeeds…it's you."

I chewed my lip before saying, "I need your help. I never ask for it. But I'm asking for it now…please."

"What is it that you need?"

"To know what to do. How do I help? I feel so useless right now."

"Ah, so nothing big."

I smirked. "Finding the Relics was one thing. It was a clear task. I knew the end goal. But right now, I feel lost. I'm here in the Otherwhere as long as you need me. I'm willing to give everything I have to this fight. But I don't know what to do. I don't understand why the Lightsmith is threatening us. I feel desperate, and there are days when Callum goes off to meet with leaders to strategize…and I'm here, alone, at my wits' end. Waiting, helpless, not knowing what my job is."

"I see."

Merriwether waved a hand in the air, and the Orb vanished.

He stepped over and laid a hand on my shoulder, slouching down to look into my eyes. "You, Vega, have incredible instincts. You always have. They've saved you many times. They've saved all of us, in fact. So, my advice to you is follow your instincts. Don't sit around the Academy if you feel you can make yourself useful elsewhere."

"I'm not an army," I said. "I can't just venture out into the Otherwhere and take on the enemy."

"Perhaps not. But you *can* make new friends—and reacquaint yourself with those who are already close to you."

8

OLD FRIENDS

I DECIDED TO TAKE MERRIWETHER'S ADVICE AND PAY A VISIT TO someone I knew well.

Unfortunately, it was also someone who probably wished me a million miles away.

When I left my grandfather's office, I transported myself to the Aradia Coven, to the street just outside Solara's front door. I stood there a moment, my hands shaking as I contemplated who I might find inside.

Solara was a powerful Witch, head of the Coven and descendant of Morgan Le Fay. She was a friend, though when I'd first met her, I'd found her somewhat daunting…to put it mildly. But it wasn't only her I was here to see.

I wanted to see Lachlan, too.

I hadn't seen him since our goodbye after our altercation when my summoned flame soldiers had nearly killed him. I had no idea whether he'd grown to despise me since then, or if we could somehow pick up the brittle pieces of the friendship we'd once shared and twist them back together.

So much had happened to us both since the days when we'd first met. We had traveled many miles together. We'd grown close. We had fought bitterly. We'd saved one another…and nearly ended one another.

So, when I raised my fist and rapped on Solara's door, I found myself trembling in anticipation of seeing Lachlan's familiar face.

More often than not, Solara's door sprang open in greeting when I arrived for unannounced visits. But this time, I had to wait a few seconds before I heard hurried footsteps approach.

"Vega," Solara breathed as she opened the door, drawing me in for a hard hug. "It's so good to see you. Come inside, will you?"

"It's good to see you, too," I said, trying to mask my unease as I followed her into the house.

"Sit," she said, guiding me into her cozy kitchen. "I'm just making tea. I'll pour you a cup."

"Where's Lachlan?" I asked, taking a seat by the window and peering out.

"Around." The answer was more vague than I expected, and I eyed Solara curiously. She looked tired, particularly for someone who normally exuded extraordinary strength and power.

"Are you all right?" My voice was tight, as was my chest. Seeing her like this felt like a bad omen.

"I'm fine," she said. "I'm afraid we've had some bad news from the mountains. There have been attacks on Grells, as well as many others."

At that, my heart felt like it might explode. "Callum headed to the mountains to meet with Kohrin. Do you think—"

I couldn't bring myself to ask if he might be in danger. I couldn't bear to think about it.

Solara shook her head. "No. If he's seeing Kohrin, he'll be all right. Kohrin's family is isolated from the fighting. He's preparing to travel this way with a large force of Grells—and they're staying out of the fighting for now."

I breathed a hefty sigh of relief, trying my best to conceal how frightened I'd been.

"The battles have been raging for days now," Solara continued, "from all corners of the Otherwhere. The queen's forces are more widespread than we ever knew. Fires are breaking out spontaneously in the wilderness. Some are convinced it's Lumus who is wreaking havoc from the shadows—and each day, the fighting moves closer to the Covens." Her voice took on a bitter tint when she added, "Not that it matters who is responsible. What matters is ending this madness."

"Of *course* it's Lumus," I said with a sneer, taking hold of the cup of spiced tea Solara handed me. She always made the most delicious tea, swirling with a thousand pleasant flavors that managed to steal my worries away, if only for a few moments at a time.

I was about to say something more when the front door swung open and I heard the familiar patter of clawed feet on the floor. I didn't need to turn around to know a certain Husky was making his way toward me, tongue out, a happy grin on his black lips.

"Niala!" I cried out, leaping to my feet and spinning around to greet my friend.

She threw her arms around me as Rourke, her Familiar, pressed his nose to my leg.

"It's been too long," she said, pulling back and turning to Solara. "I hope it's okay that we just barged in…"

Solara laughed. "Of course it is. I don't suppose you know where Lachlan is, do you?"

"Off with Lily, I think," Niala replied. Her eyes went wide and she blurted out, "Oh—I forgot. You probably don't know yet, Vega."

"Know what?" I asked, grinning, my brows shooting upward. For a moment, I forgot the war and all it entailed. "Does Lachlan have a new special friend?"

"Yeah. I mean…" Niala looked awkward, for once. She was always so self-assured, so put-together, but right now, she looked like a flustered teenager.

"She's a Witch, from the Navarre Coven," Solara offered. "She's young and in training, and she came to us a few months ago. Lachlan has been spending a good deal of time with her." She looked a little hesitant as she told me the news, as if afraid it would injure me.

I nodded. "I'm so glad to hear it," I said. "Really. Assuming she's good to him."

"She is," Solara said. "I think you'll find him somewhat changed since your last meeting. Why don't you two go find him? I have a little…work to do here."

"Are you sure you're all right?" I asked. "You seem…distracted."

Solara went silent for a second before replying, "Have you heard about the Lightsmith's presence in the Otherwhere?"

I nodded. "I have. I came here partly because I was hoping to ask you to help me seek him out. Merriwether thinks he wants to get his hands on the Relics, and we can't let that happen."

"Agreed," Solara said. "But I should tell you—the Lightsmith is more than just a destroyer of Relics. He's somewhat more dangerous than a mere force of chaos."

I threw Niala a look before asking, "What do you mean?"

Solara sighed, speaking low. "He's a thief of magic—an entity that steals from Witches, Wizards, and others. He's like a spell-vampire—one who can take from even the most powerful beings. Even someone like Merriwether, or…"

"Or Lumus," I replied.

She nodded. "If you should find him first—be careful, Vega. You can't afford to lose your abilities, and we can't afford for you to lose them. You are important in the days to come. Perhaps more than any Witch, Wizard, or dragon in the Otherwhere."

"I have no wish to get near the Lightsmith—at least, not nearer than I absolutely have to. But if I find him, what do I do? How do I keep him from taking my powers?"

"Don't let him touch you," Solara said. "And try your best not to look into his eyes. He will draw you to him if he can—and he will take everything from you. He can only be controlled if he's trapped or imprisoned. I suspect Merriwether wants him locked inside the Academy."

"Wait—" I sputtered. "The Academy? Wouldn't that be insanely dangerous for everyone there? The Relics are locked up inside!"

"I know," Solara lamented. "But the fact is, Merriwether is probably the only one on our side powerful enough to take on the Lightsmith—or at least to incapacitate him long enough for us to defeat the queen and Lumus. I wouldn't get close to him for all the gold in these lands. Not unless I had no other choice. The smith is an ancient being—one who tried to steal my ancestor's powers from her once."

"Morgan le Fay?" I asked. "Really?"

"Really. It is also said that the Lightsmith is tied to the Prophecy—the one about the heir to the throne of the Otherwhere. Though how, I don't yet know. But we need to find him. It's more important than anything else right now."

"If he wants the Relics, wouldn't he head straight for the Academy?"

"He may," Solara admitted. "But if he arrives there unannounced, who knows how many people he'll kill to gain entry. It's best if we locate him then report directly to Merriwether."

With a nod, I said, "I understand."

But the truth was, I didn't. Not really.

Why would my grandfather want such a powerful creature anywhere near the Academy?

There had to be more to this than Solara was telling me.

9

THE ARADIA COVEN

Niala led me down a series of cobbled streets until we came to a row of beautiful white houses, each unique in its way. They were made of wood with gingerbread-style architectural details, and I found my heart lightening a little more with each abode that we passed.

The air was fresh, relaxing, and pure, and for a dream-like moment I longed to be back in Fairhaven with Liv, living the simple life I had before I knew of the Otherwhere's troubles. I would have loved to find myself walking to Perks for an iced coffee or sitting in the Commons, laughing about some inane tv show or other.

I missed those simple days—the days before any of this had begun. They'd been happy ones, except, of course, for the shadow that had hung over me since my parents' death. Liv had been such a good friend, and Fairhaven was unquestionably a beautiful town. I had always lamented the fact that it was quiet and a little dull, but right now, it seemed like heaven.

Here on the cusp of war, I would have given almost anything to return to the simplicity of that former life.

"Except I would lose Callum," I said softly.

"What's that?" Niala asked.

I let out a quiet laugh. "Just talking to myself. Wishing I was back in Fairhaven, away from worries about war and pain and violence and cruel people."

"Oh, is that all?" She reached out and took my hand, squeezing before letting it go again. "I hate to break it to you, but you've always been destined to be part of this world, Vega. Scary as it is—*mad* as it is—I really believe it. You're *part* of the Otherwhere. One day, the bards will sing songs about you, and if there's an Academy in the future, its students will learn about your bravery."

"What if there's no Academy?"

Niala shrugged. "Then you'll have done your job brilliantly, I suppose."

"I almost hope the day comes soon when we don't need it anymore," I said. "The school's main purpose is to train Seekers and their helpers to find the Relics every fifty years to help stave off conflict. Imagine a time when the Relics don't matter—when they can be forgotten at long last. A time when the Otherwhere has a kind, thoughtful leader who doesn't pose a danger to his own subjects—or vice versa."

"That would only be possible if there were no one to challenge for the throne—if the ruler of the Otherwhere was well liked by everyone…which would mean no more Usurper Queen—and no more drama."

I laughed bitterly. "Maybe it's a dream that can never come true, but a girl can hope. If Callum takes the throne, the Otherwhere could finally settle into lasting peace. He's severed from Caffall. The kingdom never has to worry about him losing his mind to his dragon like the Crimson King did. Callum is exactly what the realm needs."

"True," Niala said. "But there is always the risk of a challenger to the throne, isn't there? The Academy has always existed to keep the peace—to maintain the balance of good and evil. That's what the Relics are for, after all. Maybe they'll always be needed. Maybe Seekers will still need to be trained every so often, just as they always have been."

She had a point.

There would probably always be a need for a training facility of some sort or other. Still, I had hoped no one else would have to endure what we Seekers had—what my Nana had endured too, when she was Chosen Seeker so long ago. I hoped with everything in me that there would come a time when Callum sat in his rightful place on the throne, when all was well with the Otherwhere, and when the Relics of Power could remain concealed forever.

When we arrived at the last house on our right, Niala stopped then leaned down and whispered something to Rourke, who bounded over and pawed at the door.

A moment later, it opened inward to reveal Lachlan grinning down at the Husky, offering up a pat on his head. At first, he didn't see me, and I had the pleasure of watching him in his natural state.

He was rosy cheeked, and he even looked…

Happy.

It wasn't until he pulled his eyes to mine that his smile faded. He shot bolt upright, a look I couldn't quite figure out overtaking his eyes.

"Vega," he said awkwardly, running a hand through his thick hair.

"Lachlan," I replied, slightly amused at the formality of his posture. "How are you?"

"I…" he began, then stopped and tried again. "I…"

As if summoned by his inability to speak, a figure appeared next to him. A young woman of eighteen or nineteen, her hair was red, her eyes green. She was exceedingly pretty, and something about her seemed to shine as if she were her own light source.

"You must be Lily," I said, stepping forward and ignoring the uneasy look on Lachlan's face. "I'm Vega."

She held out a hand and I took it, shaking it heartily. "Vega, at last!" she replied. "I've heard so much about you."

"All bad, I assume," I said with a smirk. "It wouldn't be entirely unfair if that was the case."

"Not bad at all," Lily replied. "I mean, unless you count the fact that Lachlan did mention you nearly killed him. I'd venture to guess he probably deserved it." With that, she elbowed Lachlan in the ribs. He flinched, then grinned.

It was so strange—but good—to see him comfortable with someone other than me.

Liv had tried so many times to convince him to become her boyfriend. And though he had tolerated it well enough, I knew how hard it had been for him to put on the façade of a regular human around her.

"To be fair," Lachlan said, "Vega wasn't the one who nearly killed me. It was those damned archers."

"Archers that I summoned," I corrected. "And I will never stop being sorry for the pain they inflicted. But I'm glad to see you looking like your old self."

Lachlan contemplated his next words carefully before saying, "If you hadn't summoned them, I don't know what would have happened to me—to either of us, honestly. I might have killed you, Vega—and I wouldn't have been able to live with myself."

The sincerity in his voice was enough to make me swallow hard, and I fought back the tears that wanted desperately to form in my eyes. Forcing them away, I clapped my hands together and said, "Right. Well—we have a war to deal with and a queen to stop before she burns this realm and everyone in it to the ground. So the fact is, I need your help."

10
LACHLAN

Lily looked from one of us to the other, then said, "I want to hear everything, but I'm afraid I have a quick errand to run for Solara. I'll be back soon, though—why don't you two catch up while I'm gone?"

She pressed a kiss to Lachlan's cheek before taking off into the sky. *Walking on the wind*, the Witches called it—it was their equivalent of flying.

The Otherwhere's Witches had destroyed every preconception I'd ever had about their kind. They never used brooms or any other means to find their way into the sky. Instead, they moved gracefully, as if slipping along on the air, itself.

It was a beautiful sight, and Lily was obviously experienced.

"She seems pretty great," I told Lachlan.

He smiled sheepishly, ran a hand through his hair again, and said, "Yeah, she is."

"Solara has told you about the rules of the Covens, I assume," I added, not wanting to rain on his parade, but worried that he might be blindsided if he learned the hard way that Witches were not to mingle romantically with others. It wasn't strictly forbidden—but according to the Coven laws, a Witch who married outside her Coven was expelled and lost her powers. It had happened to Solara's own sister, Tarrah.

"I'm aware of the rules, and so is Lily," Lachlan said. "We... well, let's just say it's a new relationship. We're not about to get married, so Solara is allowing us to spend time together. Besides which, Solara is totally preoccupied with the war."

"I can tell," I agreed. "I've never seen her like this. She seems troubled in a way that makes me nervous."

"She's worried, Vega—like we all are. She wants to protect the realm and her Sisters. But the queen's forces have already torn apart so much of the land. It's really bad out there."

I didn't have the heart to ask if he saw his relationship with Lily going anywhere or if they were simply taking it one day at a time.

There might not be too many more days left for any of us, after all.

"So," Lachlan said, gesturing to a comfortable-looking chair in the small sitting room before taking a seat himself. "Tell me—how was the end of the school year?"

I laughed, plopping down in the armchair, one leg tucked under me. "It was strange. You know, because of everything that had happened. You weren't there—that part sort of sucked. I have a reputation now as the girl who makes all the cute boys disappear."

He winced slightly with those words, and I thought about apologizing for being insensitive, but he read my mind and held up a hand. "It's okay," he said. "I didn't deserve to be around you, Vega. Especially after the things I said and did when my—"

My father. He was about to say it, but stopped himself, and I couldn't blame him. Meligant—brother to the Crimson King—wasn't exactly the parental figure Lachlan had craved all his life. He was soulless and cruel and was more than willing to use his son to further his own agenda.

"Come on, now," I said. "We both know the Lachlan who

confronted me in Meligant's hideaway was not the Lachlan I know and care about."

But my friend shook his head, and for a moment he almost looked like he might break down in tears. "He was inside me, though. He still exists somewhere deep in my soul. That's enough to tell me I was wrong all along, back when I tried more than once to convince you to care for me. I should never have put you in that position."

I waved a hand, trying to blow it off like it was nothing. "It's all forgotten," I said. "None of it matters now. We have far more important things to worry about."

But Lachlan narrowed his eyes at me. "I'm trying to apologize, Vega. I need you to accept it. I also want you to know I support and respect Callum. He's steady and strong—and, well, he's mature, as young as he may look. He's always been more worthy of you and the throne than I could ever be."

To that, I had no response. I just nodded quietly and inhaled a deep breath.

I didn't entirely relish Lachlan mentioning the throne. I didn't want to acknowledge that he was part of the succession—that if his deranged father were in any shape to do so, he would try again to steal it for himself.

Fortunately, Meligant was somewhere out in the wilds of the Otherwhere. His dragon, Mardochaios, had deserted him—probably because he treated the poor beast terribly.

"Don't worry," he said. "I mean it. I support Callum's claim. He is the rightful king. You have my word that I'll do whatever it takes to get him there."

"Thank you," I said, more relieved than I cared to admit.

"On another note—you graduated, right?" Lachlan asked. "I mean, from high school. You're a real human adult now?"

I laughed again. "Not sure about the human part. Or the adult part, for that matter. But yeah, somehow, I kept my head on straight enough to graduate. Will even came to the ceremony, which was amazing."

The truth was, my brother's presence at graduation had been wonderful. Without Callum there, I'd found myself feeling a little empty, especially given how many of my classmates had large families in attendance.

Will had been so proud of me, his smile beaming from the back of the auditorium. He'd made me feel like every sacrifice, every sleepless night, every bit of effort to keep up with my studies after all that had happened was worth it.

"I guess the trip to Fairhaven from California's not so bad when you have a sister who can summon you from your dorm room," Lachlan laughed.

"Exactly." I sighed. It had been bittersweet to see Will, ever since the drama at Christmas. He finally knew what I was, what my destiny entailed, and what it still meant for my future. The knowledge he'd gained had brought us closer over the months, even though we were apart. We spoke several times a week on the phone, or in person on the rare occasions when I popped out to California to visit. "It's become a running joke how much we both save on airfare—and how much we'll save in the future, if I stay in that world."

"*If.*" Lachlan spoke the word as though it was filled with meaning.

I nodded. "It's a big if, I'll admit. I...I also told Will about the money Merriwether gave us. Two million dollars—and I gave half to him, of course. He was a little blown away, though he warned me that in California, that barely covers a month's rent. I'm pretty sure he was joking, though."

"I can only imagine what he must have felt when he found out," Lachlan said with a low whistle. "It's life-changing, that kind of cash."

"He said it felt like the freedom to choose our own fates—and I think he was right." A wistful smile crept over my lips. "We had some really good talks about our grandfather and Nana. About the Otherwhere and Callum. But the one thing we never talked about was what I planned to do after graduation."

By some miracle, I'd finished the year on the honor roll. Between my visits to the Otherwhere, I'd worked my butt off, trying to keep my grades up while spending weekends with Callum in the Rose Wing, my mind and heart split between the coming war and my potential future in the very normal world I'd grown up in.

I had told Will of my plan to head to the Otherwhere after graduation. That I didn't know if I'd be back to Fairhaven for good, but not to worry—I would come see him often, regardless of my final choice.

What I didn't tell him was that I was terrified that my future might be filled with violence and death. I didn't mention that I feared for Callum's life now just as I had almost since the day I'd met him.

He was the primary target of too many powerful people. The queen. Lumus. Meligant.

I had even worried about Lachlan—though now, seeing him face to face, I knew at least that I didn't have to fear him. Something in him had changed. He had reverted to his old self, but calmer, somehow—like his powers had brought about a realization of what he needed in his life.

"Vega," Lachlan said, leaning toward me. He didn't try to touch me or take my hand. And for once, I wasn't afraid he'd ask me for something I couldn't give.

He simply looked into my eyes and offered up a reassuring smile. "Whatever you decide—whatever madness happens over the next days here in the Otherwhere—I swear to you that I'll help you. You won't be in this alone. The prophecy that claims the rightful heir will end up on the throne? I told you—I'll do everything I can to make sure that comes to pass."

I smiled, but my lips quickly pulled into a frown. "The

prophecy doesn't mention Callum by name. What if that heir is you?"

The words barely made it past my lips. It was impossible to say them without sounding as if I was offering up some sort of accusation. *What if you want to steal the throne? What if you kill Callum and take it for yourself?*

What if your awful father challenges Callum's claim?

But that wasn't what I meant.

What if Lachlan, by virtue of being part of the Crimson King's bloodline, had some claim that we didn't know about?

"I don't aspire to the throne," Lachlan said, a hint of frost in his voice. "I don't want to be king."

"Only a true madman would *want* to be king," I replied. "It's so much…I don't know, responsibility. The Otherwhere has so many creatures in it, so much conflict. So much that needs fixing. I wouldn't wish that duty on anyone. Not you, not Callum."

"If Callum manages to take the throne, Vega, I promise—I'll help him in any way he needs. He won't be alone. But will you be by his side? His queen?"

I lowered my eyes to look down at the ring on my finger, twisting it around nervously.

"I want to help this place," I said. "I love this land. Everything about it. The Witches. The dragons. The Grells. The people. Merriwether." I pulled my eyes up to meet his but didn't add, "You." Still, I hoped he understood. "But there's still a part of me that's scared to abandon my former life. Will, Liv—I need them. And I think they need me."

"You wouldn't have to shut yourself away from them, surely. You could live here and visit there often."

"But here, I wouldn't age the same way. I'm a magic-user here. There, I'm just a person. If Will marries one day and has children—how will he explain their very young-looking aunt?"

"Anti-aging cream?"

At that, I snickered. "Touché."

"Point is, you'll figure it out. You may be a gifted magic user—there are some who still call you Sorcière around here—but you're also Vega the problem-solver, and you always have been. It's what you do best. You figure out how to fix things."

I sighed. "I don't know if I can fix this, Lachlan."

"Fix what?" he asked, leaning in closer. There was a look of concern in his expression. "Vega—why are you really here?"

"I told you—I wanted to see how you were doing," I insisted, but Lachlan rolled his eyes at me.

"You do realize I know you pretty damned well, don't you, Sloane?" he asked with a dry chuckle. "That's not the only reason you're here. I can feel the tension coming off you—and something else, too. Fear."

"Am I that transparent?"

"I mean, you *are* a Shadow—or have you forgotten you can pretty well disappear from view?"

I laughed. "I haven't forgotten—but it's not a power I like to use very often. And I have no intention of hiding myself away while we deal with our new enemy."

"New enemy?" Lachlan raised a brow. "Do I dare ask what you mean?"

"We're looking for someone called the Lightsmith," I told him. "He's a powerful being of intense magic who wants to destroy the Relics. If he does, our side may lose our strength and our advantage. I really did come here to check in on you, Lachlan—but I'm also hoping the Witches of the Aradia Coven can help."

11
BAD TIDINGS

"Come on, then," Lachlan said, leaping to his feet. "Let's go figure out how to find this Lightsmith guy."

I smirked, pushed myself up off the chair, and said, "If you insist." I tried to sound casual, even playful, but the truth was, the thought of the Lightsmith still terrified me. Solara's fear was enough to remind me this was no mere Waerg we were dealing with. The Lightsmith was strong in ways I hadn't even begun to imagine.

"I'll walk you back to Solara's," Lachlan offered, no doubt sensing the tension in the air.

I nodded and followed him out of the house.

As we walked, he asked how Callum was doing.

"He's...preoccupied," I said. "He's got a lot of weight on his shoulders right now. *Too* much. But he's holding his head up high, as always. Acting like the leader he was born to be."

"You know, it's so strange," Lachlan said.

"What is?"

"Realizing after all this time that I have a cousin. One who made me so angry for so long for being so close to perfect."

"Um, what do you mean, *'close to'*?" I asked with a snicker.

"Fine. He's perfect and dreamy," Lachlan said, rolling his eyes and kicking a stone along the street. "And I did a terrible job of accepting how much you cared about him—of accepting what a good person he is, Vega. I'm so sorry for all of it."

I waved a hand and said, "Forget it. It's old news," but Lachlan grabbed my arm, stopping me in my tracks, and turned me his way.

"No, I mean it," he said. "You were the closest thing to family that I've ever had. Despite the Waerg pack raising me and everything else, you felt like someone I could trust. Someone I could love like my own kin. I'd never had that, and I let it take me over and break me in ways I didn't even know were possible. You never deserved to be on the receiving end of my trauma."

I looked down at his hand on my arm, and he pulled away, interpreting my staring as a reprimand. But I reached for his shoulder and said, "You lost your mother. You were taken out of your world and put somewhere far away from your relatives, Lachlan. You lived your whole life in the wrong place—in the wrong *time*, even. It's a miracle how well-adjusted you are. I'm just glad you're able to see Callum now for what he is. I only hope maybe, someday, you two can become as close as I know you can. You both matter so much to me—and I know you've never felt satisfied with that, but it's the truth. I care a lot about you." I swallowed hard before adding, "One of the most devastating things that ever happened to me was having to hurt you. And I don't just mean the archers."

He frowned, nodded, and said, "Yeah, I get it. I know you care about me, and I was selfish to deny how much of a gift that was—and still is. Your friendship is everything. I see that now."

"Callum has had his share of trauma, too," I said. "You have it in common. You were taken from this world and left somewhere strange and frightening in your youth—and he was imprisoned and abused by his own twisted parents. Who knows? Maybe someday, you two will bond over all of it."

"Or go mad together from the after-effects," Lachlan said. With a snicker, he added, "Oh, wait. I guess I already did that."

"Meligant did that to you," I said with a shudder, recalling what Lachlan's father—a dead-eyed, psychotic monster—had done to him in Fairhaven. Thrusting Lachlan's powers on him without any kind of preparation, which had overwhelmed Lachlan's mind and body to the point where he didn't know himself anymore.

"Meligant is long gone," he said, refusing to call the cruel monster his father. "He's probably hiding out in the mountains while poor Mardochaios licks his wounds."

"I do feel for that dragon," I lamented as we began to walk again. "He never deserved a fate like the one that was thrust on him."

Solara wasn't home when we arrived, so we let ourselves in and took over her couch, plopping down to slouch lazily while we waited for her return.

We had been sitting and talking for a half hour or so when Solara showed up with Lily. Both of them were breathless, and from the looks on their faces, they were deeply concerned.

"We've found him," Lily said. "The Witches of the Maraud Coven have spotted the Lightsmith. He's heading east through the foothills and making his way toward the Academy. He's probably mere hours from reaching its gates."

I shot a look at Lachlan, then at Solara. "What do we do?"

Solara grimaced. "We have no choice but to go to him," she said. "Before it's too late. The Witches of the Maraud Coven know he's dangerous, but they don't know what he's capable of. Their leader, Clio, is powerful but stubborn as all hell. I need to tell her what she's up against before it's too late."

12
A PLAN

I CONTEMPLATED SUMMONING CALLUM BUT DECIDED AGAINST IT.

If he was strategizing with Kohrin and the other Grells about the coming battle, their time was better served finishing the job than being torn away to fight one being—even one as destructive as the Lightsmith.

After all, if Witches weren't enough to take on the Lightsmith, I couldn't imagine who was.

It didn't take long for our party of four to get ready—including Lily, who had changed into an outfit of form-fitting black leather pants and boots, a white shirt, and a red jacket.

I exchanged a quick look with Lachlan, who glanced back at me with a shrug as if to say, "What can I tell you? She's a badass."

Solara asked Niala to stay behind with Rourke to stand guard over the Coven.

"What if someone needs healing?" Niala asked.

Solara shook her head. "The Lightsmith doesn't simply injure people. He steals their lives as well as their magic. There will be no use for a Healer, not where we're going."

I shuddered as I looked out toward the edge of the Coven and the great unknown that lay beyond.

"I can fly you, Vega," Lachlan said. "I assume you don't Wind-Walk like the others."

I'd almost forgotten that he now possessed far more power than a mere Waerg. When Meligant had tortured him in the Commons in Fairhaven, Lachlan had altered and turned into a number of different creatures—which meant he was now a fully-fledged shapeshifter. And it seemed that he'd learned to control the power while staying with the Witches.

I glanced at Lily, who nodded her approval. "He's especially talented at turning into a drake," she said. "A fire drake, to be precise. He's quite handsome with his scales on."

"A *drake*, you say?" I asked with a smile. "Interesting."

"I know, I know," Lachlan replied with a roll of his eyes. "It's Callum's last name. We *are* cousins, don't forget—which means it could well be my name, too. Not that Meligant has ever told me he actually calls himself by any surname. You may be surprised to hear he and I don't engage in a lot of father-son days at the park."

"Still," I said, chuckling. "It seems you and Callum have more in common than you ever knew. So, you're really okay if I…"

"I already said you can have a ride," Lachlan said, then quickly glanced at Lily and added, "I mean, if it's okay with you."

"Totally fine," she said, and I smiled to see her confidence when she took his hand and planted a kiss on his cheek. She winked when she said, "I promise not to get jealous, as long as you promise to protect her."

You have no reason to be jealous, Lily, I thought, watching Lachlan's eyes on her. *He obviously cares about you. I think he may even love you.*

Lachlan distanced himself from us, moving away from Solara's house to shift into a narrow dragon with a long, arching neck. His wings were folded neatly against his body, his large and shapely feet were accented by sharp talons.

He was much smaller than Caffall, but still big enough to be intimidating. He was at least the size of a large draught horse, his scales a glimmering crimson.

As his wings unfurled elegantly, I wondered for a moment if Lachlan was happy about this development. The life of a Waerg was all he'd ever known until a short time ago, and now a whole new world had opened to him.

I just wished his abilities hadn't been forced on him in such a violent, cruel manner.

When he pushed his head to the ground to make my climb easier, I slipped over to him and hesitated for only a moment before I leapt up onto his back, grateful for the ride. Even if I could Walk on the Wind as the Witches did, I wasn't sure I'd be able to keep up with them. They moved like the air itself, slipping along as if each of them weighed less than a feather.

"We need to go," Solara said, leading the way toward the sky, her feet moving as though she were simply striding along the ground.

Lily followed, and then Lachlan surged into the air with a sharp cry. I held onto the mane of spiky scales jutting up from his neck, grateful for the feeling of security they offered.

Despite everything that had gone on between Lachlan and me, I trusted him completely. I knew how loyal he was, and how good. He would not let me fall—and he would protect me with his life if it came down to it.

But something told me he wouldn't be able to help me in the confrontation that lay ahead.

No one would.

13
TO THE ROAD

On the many occasions when I'd ridden Caffall, I always felt as though I was seated on a broad couch, secure as anything.

But Lachlan's drake was narrower, and as we soared upward, the trees below us growing smaller and smaller, I grew far less confident that I could keep my seat. My weight shifted left and right, my legs unable to hold onto his sleek scales hard enough to instill confidence.

~*Don't worry*, a familiar but gravelly voice spoke to my mind as I struggled to keep myself upright while long wings beat at the air to either side of me. *I won't let anything happen to you.*

"I appreciate it," I replied, my eyes fixed on the landscape in the distance, the Otherwhere's rolling green hills welcoming and daunting at once. Somewhere beyond them lay our enemy—and to all sides, no doubt, were hundreds of Waergs and Ursals wreaking havoc on the lands.

As we flew, I recalled what Solara had warned.

"Don't let him touch you," I said softly.

~*Are you trying to tell me something?* Lachlan's voice replied. *Because I have no intention of going anywhere near that psychopath.*

I chuckled. "I wasn't talking to you. I was just reminding

myself what Solara said about the smith. She warned me he can steal powers—so you need to make sure to keep your distance from him, too."

~Fine. But how are we supposed to incapacitate him if none of us can get near him?

"We'll have to wing it."

~Wing it, Lachlan said with an extra-aggressive flap of his broad wings. *Very clever.*

"Yeah, I'm a freaking genius. Anyhow, we're spell-casters, right? I'm sure between us, we can figure it out."

We traveled surprisingly fast, and we'd flown for only twenty minutes or so when Solara called out, "There he is," pointing toward the lands to the east of where we now soared.

Far below, heading toward the Academy—which was little more than a tiny spot in the far distance—I could see a glowing figure moving swiftly along the road.

He wore a cloak of silvery-white, a glow radiating from every inch of him.

"He shines like the sun," I recalled the boy Davith saying when we'd questioned him.

Indeed, he shone. But he had none of the sun's warmth about him. Instead, he felt ice-cold and terrifying, his movements strange and unnatural. It reminded me too much of a snake, despite the fact that he had legs and arms. At first, he appeared to be entirely alone, with no one else around for miles.

It was as though he had convinced his route to clear itself to allow him easy access to the Academy.

But as we began our descent, four figures appeared on the road before the Lightsmith. Smoke and mist swirled around their feet in a striking display of power and beauty.

Witches of the Maraud Coven.

"Solara!" I cried out.

"I see them," she called back. "Don't get any closer—not yet."

On her command, Lachlan halted in the air, his wings beating slowly as we readied ourselves to watch the drama unfold on the ground.

I wanted to protest—to tell Solara we needed to land. But she looked so intent on protecting her fellow Witches that I couldn't bring myself to offer her yet another distraction.

"Damn it, Clio," she snarled. "You stubborn fool!"

Something ignited in Solara then. She surged downward, aiming for the road behind the enemy. She'd almost landed when the Lightsmith twisted around to face her.

His golden eyes, devoid of irises and pupils, flared bright with what looked like licking flames. His skin was glistening white, almost translucent, as though he'd never encountered daylight.

"Stay back, Witch," his voice hissed on the air, sharp as an arrow. "Do not come any closer or your life will end."

He narrowed his terrifying eyes at Solara for only a few seconds before turning back to the Witches blocking the road.

It took a moment to realize Solara was frozen in place, her feet dangling a foot or so above the ground. He had done this to her—cast a spell that even a Witch of her skills couldn't break.

Lily glided over to hang in the air next to Lachlan, a hand pressed to his neck. I could feel her fear as acutely as my own to see such an overwhelming entity down below—one who already seemed too powerful for any of us to confront.

I don't blame you, I thought. *I'm scared, too.*

As my gaze moved back to the scene unfolding below us—to the Lightsmith, stopped in his tracks, and the four Witches standing before him, their arms outspread to form a blockade—I knew we were already too late.

A Witch in red took a step forward, raising her chin to take in Solara and the rest of us. Her expression was one of pride, of defiance.

A sick feeling inside me told me there was an unspoken rivalry between her and the head of the Aradia Coven.

"He may think he can take me," her voice bellowed on the air. "But I'm stronger."

"You're not, Clio!" Solara shouted, her voice desperate. "You *must* back away from him!"

The Witch called Clio threw her head back and laughed as if the very suggestion was utterly absurd. "You always did think me a weakling, Solara," she said. "I know how to handle this one."

"Oh, God," I said. "She doesn't know what he can do…"

She took a step toward the Lightsmith, and Solara, freed suddenly from whatever spell he'd cast, surged down and landed some distance behind him. She strode toward him, a hand extended—and I could feel her power on the air as she conjured a spell to take him down.

He spun around, and after one quick flick of his hand, Solara was frozen again. This time, her body contorted painfully as the Lightsmith pivoted to move toward Clio and her companions, who looked as defiant as their leader.

"Lachlan," I said frantically. "We need to stop him!"

I didn't need to utter any more words before he pulled free of Lily's touch and swooped downward, his speed increasing dramatically as we flew toward the glowing figure in the road.

As if to let me know my help wasn't needed, Clio took another step toward the Lightsmith, a hand raised in the air, palm out as she confronted him.

"I will burn you, bastard!" she cried, her voice shrill and menacing.

But as he slipped toward her, her expression changed from one of confidence to one of confusion.

Her spell wasn't working.

"Stop," she commanded, "or my Sisters and I will tear you to shreds!"

A strange, cold laugh rose through the air, and I knew without a doubt that Clio had already lost this battle.

14
CONFRONTATION

"We can't let him touch Clio!" I cried. "He'll kill her!"

I could feel that Lachlan was giving everything inside him to hurtle his drake toward the ground far below us—but he lacked the gift of Caffall's tremendous speed.

"Can you shoot a fireball at him?" I asked. "Throw him a distraction?"

~*It would be too dangerous,* he lamented. *Solara and the others are too close.*

A sudden, sickening realization assaulted me as I watched the Lightsmith slither forward with his strange, inhuman gait:

We were too far away to help the Witches.

"Lachlan," I said, leaning in close. "Don't freak out, but I'm going down there."

~*What?* Lachlan's voice snapped inside my head. *Vega, don't you dare!*

But by the time the last word traveled from his mind to my own, I had vanished from his back.

I was on the ground a moment later, my feet planted on the road just a few feet behind the Lightsmith. Solara was behind me, still twisted in agony, frozen and struggling against the brutal magic holding her in place.

"Vega," she managed to say, the words forcing themselves out from between clenched teeth. "Don't."

"I have to do something!" I told her over my shoulder before calling to the Lightsmith. "Smith—don't hurt them! Please!"

Fear chilled me to the bone when the entity twisted around to stare at me with those cold, unblinking eyes.

"Do not try to stop me, Daughter of Viviane," he said. His eerie voice trailed along my skin like a hostile, long-legged creature.

I knew I wasn't supposed to get too close to him. But something was drawing me in, forcing me to step forward and examine him more closely.

He seemed entirely crafted of light, of something pure, yet terribly dangerous—something tinged with mischief and mayhem.

I understood, as my eyes moved over him, that he was a creature of pure fundamental magic. The magic that existed at the world's birth—magic that had never been tamed or harnessed but lived wild on the air.

"Why have you shown yourself after all this time?" I asked, my voice a quiver. "Have you come to destroy the Relics of Power? Did the queen send you?"

The Lightsmith looked almost amused by the questions—if someone with such an expressionless face could look amused. "I serve no master and no mistress. My reasons for coming are my own, and you will understand them soon enough."

I fought the desire to move still closer, reminding myself just how dangerous he was.

I'll cast a spell when he turns back around. I'll shield the Witches from him. But if I try it now, he'll freeze me like he did to Solara.

"I can't let you near the Relics," I said, hoping to distract him long enough for Clio to make a move. I had no idea how strong she was, but if she could just get one spell off—if she could hurt him just enough to free Solara, we might stand a chance. "We need them to fight the Usurper Queen—we *need* the prophecy to come true, for the good of this realm. Don't you see?"

Behind the smith, Clio stepped forward, as did her companions.

Without looking, the smith jutted out a hand and stopped her and her Sisters in their tracks.

"You are determined to see the rightful heir on the throne," the Lightsmith said, repeating the words of the prophecy. "But did you ever stop to think that perhaps the rightful heir already wears the crown?"

He tilted his head to the side when he added, "Or...perhaps the prophecy has been misunderstood all this time."

"Misunderstood?" I asked, trying to conceal the fear in my voice. "What do you mean?"

"The heir will one day claim what is rightfully his, they say," the strange, hollow voice replied. "But what, exactly, *is* rightfully his?"

He was speaking in riddles now, and it made no sense. "The throne," I said. "Don't play games with me, Lightsmith."

He smiled, his lips bluish against his white skin. "A throne is nothing but a seat. It is a symbol, but in the end, it is nothing. A *true* leader doesn't care for thrones, but for his people. I wish for this land to return to its former, natural state, so I am here to make sure the Otherwhere understands what sort of leadership it needs."

I let out a quiet breath of relief.

If he meant what he was saying, then surely he had no intention of allowing the Usurper Queen to keep her place on the throne. *She* wanted nothing but death and destruction.

"You have to be talking about Callum," I said. "He's clearly the only one who's destined to lead."

"The *only* one? Are you certain?" the Lightsmith laughed.

"Open your mind, Vega Sloane. Learn that the world is changing. Things are not so simple as they once were." Turning away, he spoke again. "Now, be still and keep quiet. I have work to do."

With that, he turned back to face the Witches who were struggling against his spell, the whites of their eyes betraying their fear.

I tried to speak—to shout a warning to the Witches to keep still and let him pass.

But I discovered with a shock of pain that the Lightsmith's command to be quiet had shackled my mind and body, holding me in place just as his spell had frozen the Witches. When I tried to open my mouth, I failed, my voice a mere squeak caught in my throat.

Behind me, I heard Lily and Lachlan land, feet and talons scattering gravel as they came to a skidding halt.

"Stay where you are, you two!" Solara growled. "Do not go near him! He's more powerful than I thought!"

As if taunting her and the rest of us, the Lightsmith raised a hand in the air and released Clio from his spell.

"Let's see if your Sister is sensible enough to heed that warning," he called over his shoulder to Solara.

Clio stumbled forward, an angry sneer forming on her lips as she neared him.

"I can take him down," she cried with a surprising amount of arrogance. Long, black hair swept around her beautiful face as she lowered her chin and once again thrust her hands forward, palms out, and shot a twisting array of inky black tendrils at the Lightsmith.

The strands of darkness coiled themselves around his torso, braiding through the air like thick rope.

In an instant, the enemy's arms were pinned to his sides.

Relief flooded me. Clio had succeeded in ensnaring him. We had only to get him to the Academy now—to hand him over to Merriwether, who would no doubt lock him away for good.

I tried to step forward, but to my surprise the smith's spell still held me fast, strong as ever.

If he's able to hold me here, I thought, *then he can't possibly be incapacitated.*

Sure enough, after only a few seconds spent struggling against Clio's spell, the Lightsmith managed to pull his arms from his sides. As if he were tearing paper, he pulled the black tendrils apart and leapt forward, a sudden, horrifying bolt of fury.

He cried out as he took hold of Clio, his pale hands wrapping themselves around her throat.

She tried to shove her palms out again, struggling to summon another spell. But impossibly strong fingers dug into her throat, squeezing the life out of her even as her Sisters looked on, helpless.

From where I stood frozen, I could only guess that his eyes were locked on her own as she tried to cry out.

But the only sound we heard was a silent struggle between predator and prey. And before we knew it, it was over.

When the Lightsmith had completed his task, he tossed Clio's limp body to the ground and turned to look in my direction.

The other Witches remained paralyzed, but Solara somehow managed to free herself of the Lightsmith's magic. She surged forward on the air, leaping past me to run at him, a spell of fiery lightning surging from her fingertips.

I had never seen rage on anyone's face like I saw on hers as I spun around to issue a warning. Even the Lightsmith, who seemed incapable of fear, looked momentarily shocked as Solara's brutal spell collided with his flesh, tearing a long gash in his snow-white face and neck.

Smoke rose from his skin as the smell of seared meat filled the air.

He took a long step toward Solara, whose ire reflected in his terrifying eyes as he reached a bone-white hand for her. Thinking better of it, she hurled herself backwards and out of his reach, moving like a sudden gust of fierce wind, her eyes glowing bright.

"I will kill you for what you did!" she snarled, pacing like a wildcat on the side of the road. "Make no mistake—I will end you, smith."

Raising her hands in the air, she prepared to fire off another spell.

"End me?" he asked with a low, awful chortle of amusement. "I can't be ended, Witch, unless it is by my own hand."

Angered still more by those words, Solara hurled a bolt of flame. But the Lightsmith thrust out a hand and caught it easily, curling the fire into a sphere that spun above his palm as if it were nothing but a plaything.

"Tsk," he said, laughing gently now—a disturbing sound that sent a stinging shiver of ice along my skin. "You were friends with the dead Witch, Solara, Daughter of Morgana. You *must* have known her powers. She was adept at trapping others' spells and using them for her own means. And now, her power is mine."

"I know her powers as well as my own, wretch," Solara snarled. But even now, I could see how defeated she felt.

He knew who she was. He knew her ancestry.

No doubt he knew her every weakness, too.

A renewed fear surged through me as I stared at our enemy, who was toying with the orb of fire in his hand, playing at it with his fingertips as if it was nothing more than a wad of dough.

"What do you think, Seeker?" he asked, locking his eyes on mine. "Should I burn the Witch? Would it amuse you?"

"No one should harm Witches," I snarled, struggling to free myself of his spell. "You're a magic-user. You should know better than to steal from others or take their lives. I thought you were out to protect this realm. The Witches are here to do the same."

"Fewer Witches would be a good start to a new world," he spat, his terrifying eyes landing once again on Solara. "Their kind has always hated me, and I would be only too glad to be rid of them."

He raised his arm, pulling it backwards as though to hurl the fireball.

Solara, meanwhile, was breathing hard, rage forcing her shoulders to heave.

"No, please!" I shouted, commanding as the Lightsmith's power crackled on the air and Solara readied herself to attack. "Stop!"

But I was too late.

15

THE WIZARD

Consumed by wild rage, Solara leapt at the Lightsmith.

But even as she moved, a blinding flash cut through the air, obscuring Solara, the Lightsmith, and everything else from view.

Without a second thought, I knew this flash had not come from the smith, but from someone else entirely.

Free of the enemy's paralytic spell, I threw my arm over my eyes. I was too disoriented to move, though I wanted desperately to reach for Solara and pull her back.

"Lightsmith! Cease this madness at once!"

The voice that bellowed the words was not Solara's or Lachlan's—nor was it any Witch's.

As the brightness slowly faded, a familiar figure stepped out before us, a silver cane held tight in one hand. He wore a purple waistcoat, his long limbs looking more spindly than ever. His long eyebrows were almost substantial enough to shade his eyes from the sun high above us.

I braced myself, terrified to see my grandfather in the presence of such a cruel, powerful being.

Yet some part of me was curious to see what Merriwether

would do—how his abundant strength and magic skills could take on this foe.

Solara had assured me he would be the best possible magic-user to deal with the smith. Whether or not I knew it to be true, I had no choice right now but to put my faith in him.

The Lightsmith's golden eyes narrowed and his body hunched like a predatory animal as he focused on Merriwether.

Except that *this* animal seemed jittery and daunted by his prey.

"Get out of my way, *Wizard*," he hissed.

"I will not," Merriwether replied. "You have killed a Witch. You know perfectly well that such an egregious sin has a cost. You know the laws of these lands."

"Laws?" The Lightsmith let out a croaking laugh. "You have stolen what was never yours. The Relics of Power do not belong to you or that institution filled with over-eager children. Yet you and your kind have greedily snatched them up and hoarded them over and over again for centuries. Do not speak to me of laws and sin, Mer. You have no respect for either."

Mer.

I'd never heard anyone call my grandfather by a shortened version of his name. It felt so...disrespectful. Egregious, coming from such a creature.

"We in the Academy offer the Relics refuge. We protect them from those who would use them for ill," Merriwether said, his voice a strange, booming growl unlike anything I had ever heard from a human or a beast. "I am the Relics' temporary warden, nothing more. My Seekers and I have stolen nothing. But *you* are a thief of magic and a murderer—two crimes I cannot easily forgive."

"You are wrong about me. But your Seekers? *They* are thieving monsters," the Lightsmith hissed, ignoring the accusation. "Over the years, they have stolen the Relics far too often from their hiding places—and at every turn, you have denied the Lightsmith his blood-right. It is time you let me at the objects. For too long, they've been used to wreak havoc on these lands and to drive a wedge between its people."

"If you destroy the Relics of Power," Merriwether said, raising his cane into the air and pointing it at the smith, "you will grant the advantage to our enemy. You are not supposed to take sides, smith. You are not meant to help the Usurper Queen to victory."

The Lightsmith narrowed his otherworldly, frightening eyes again and spat, "She is not *my* enemy. I have no stake in this war, and I take no sides. All I have is a task. For centuries, it has fallen on my shoulders. You and those who came before you have impeded me at every turn. It is time now for me to fulfill my destiny at long last. I am starving for it, and you deprive me of life."

"You may well have a destiny," Merriwether said. "But so do I and many others in this world. I intend to see those destinies fulfilled."

"So be it!"

With that, the Lightsmith let out a cry. His clothing glowing suddenly with dancing white flames, he shot toward my grandfather. But before he could reach him, he froze, his body contorted horribly as it began to rise toward the sky.

Merriwether's hand was in the air, the powerful spell keeping his foe at bay.

I had always known my grandfather was strong. Callum and others had assured me repeatedly that he was the most powerful of Wizards and a formidable magic user.

But I had never seen him in a situation quite like this. I had never seen him confronted by a being of pure malice and using all his strength to fight it back.

He was a warrior now—and he was ready to die to ensure our side's victory. He was willing to die to protect the Witches, Lachlan, and me.

The Lightsmith wriggled and writhed under the tight grip of

Merriwether's mind, his flesh glowing brighter now as his power amplified itself inside him.

Terror filled me to think our foul enemy might break free of the spell.

He could hurt Merriwether.

He could...*kill him.*

"No!" I screamed as another burst of light filled the air. This time, the smith freed himself of Merriwether's hold and crashed down to earth. Merriwether staggered backwards, temporarily unsteady on his feet.

The two stood facing one another, chests heaving, arms at their sides. The intensity of their stare was almost too much to take in.

"Leave us!" Merriwether cried, hurling a dark spell at his enemy.

I knew his command was aimed not at the smith, but the rest of us, but I didn't budge.

"Go now, all of you!" he barked. "Do not make me force you!"

With that, another flash came—but this time, it was followed by a profound darkness that engulfed and disoriented us.

"Vega!" This time, it was Solara who cried out, her hand grabbing my arm gently. "We need to do as your grandfather asked."

All I could see now, through the thick mass of inky blackness, was the vague outline of my grandfather and the Lightsmith. Spells exploded through the twisting air, briefly illuminating their faces as they raged, their magic fierce and violent.

Each of them dodged the other's spells adeptly before casting another attack, and another.

"But—" I began to protest, but I could see Solara's face now, lit up by the wild magic exploding so close to us.

Concern and sadness had overtaken her beautiful features, and I knew in that instant that it pained her to leave Merriwether as much as it pained me.

Solara was as powerful and strong as anyone I'd ever met. But right now, she was taking on the role of a protector, not a fighter. She would do whatever it took to keep more Witches from dying, to protect her nephew.

To protect *me*.

With a curt, reluctant nod, I turned and raced toward Lachlan's drake who was standing nearby, next to Lily and ready to soar. The Witches of the Maraud Coven had already slung their leader's lifeless body onto the drake's back.

"We'll burn her in accordance with our laws," Solara called out as a deafening explosion rang through the air. "But we need to go. Now!"

The moment I was safely on the drake's back, he shot into the air along with the Witches of the Aradia and Maraud Covens, taking care to keep Clio's body from slipping.

She won't fall, Lachlan's voice said into my mind. *I won't let her.*

"I know."

As we climbed, I turned to look over my shoulder at the terrifying display still unfolding on the ground. Through the dark smoke, all I could see were horrifying flashes of the brutal spells still shooting back and forth. It was like watching a lightning storm unfold from above the clouds—only this was far more destructive and frightening than any storm I'd ever witnessed.

"We can't just leave Merriwether to fight alone!" I cried, terrifyingly aware that I could lose my grandfather at any moment.

"Merriwether is more skilled than you know, Vega," Solara called out, her voice taking on a commanding calmness. "He has fought more powerful enemies and survived. He'll be all right."

"But what if he's not?" I snapped. "What if...if the Lightsmith kills him?"

Solara couldn't hide the quiet rage in her face when she replied, "Then we will avenge him. We'll tear the smith limb from limb...and then we'll move on to the Usurper Queen."

16
REGRETS

CONCEALING HER EMOTIONS BEHIND AN EXPRESSIONLESS MASK, Solara flew ahead.

I knew the pain she must have been feeling—the sense of loss that had struck her like a blade to the chest when the Lightsmith had killed a fellow Witch.

I understood, too, why we were retreating—why she was leading us away from the extraordinary danger the Lightsmith posed to us all. She was taking charge and protecting us, as her role of leader dictated.

The Maraud Coven's Witches would need her support in the coming hours as they laid their Sister to rest. Lily, too, would need her guidance. She was young, and for all I knew, she'd never watched one of her own die.

The last thing I wanted was to complicate Solara's life or to defy her. I was tempted to be obedient and continue on to the Aradia Coven. I could have submitted and done as Solara wished, and I would no doubt have remained safe.

But if there was one thing I'd learned over the last year, it was that I wasn't always such a good follower.

Part of me wanted to lead, too, and *all* of me wished to protect.

I wasn't willing to lose someone I loved—not if there was a single thing I could possibly do to help them.

Right now, all I could think was that my grandfather needed me.

He was in danger, and I had abandoned him.

As I clung to the drake's back behind the fallen Witch's body—a grim reminder of what the Lightsmith was capable of—I leaned forward and told Lachlan, "I'm sorry."

~*Vega?* His voice was a warning, growling deep and wild inside my mind. *What are you going to do?*

"Make things right."

~*Don't you dare. Solara will kill you if you go back there—that is, if the Lightsmith doesn't do it first.*

"It's a chance I'm willing to take."

~*No! You—*

But I didn't hear his next words.

I vanished from his back, traveling instantly to the place where we'd left Merriwether and the Lightsmith.

Only, when I arrived…they were gone.

17
RELIEF

ALL THAT REMAINED IN THE MIDDLE OF THE ROAD WAS A CRATER OF blackened earth, the grass and weeds surrounding it charred beyond recognition.

"Merriwether!" I tried to scream his name, but it came out in little more than a gasp—a frail thing, cracking at its edges and threatening to fall to earth.

I had seldom felt so alone, so helpless, or so terrified.

When our parents had died, at least I'd had Will by my side every step of the way. But now, my brother was a whole world away. Callum was in the mountains with Caffall, and Lachlan and the Witches had no choice but to return to the Coven.

I was on my own—and it was entirely possible that one of the last remaining members of my family had just left this world forever.

I couldn't fathom what I would do without Merriwether. What *anyone* in the Academy would do.

We needed our fearless leader now, more than we ever had.

I stared through tear-filled eyes at the blackened ground, at the circle of what looked like soot and char, and, horrified, wondered if the Lightsmith really could have gotten the better of the Academy's beloved Headmaster.

If he had, I would have no choice but to find him and destroy him, whatever it took.

I would not let him get away with this.

To think I'd seen Callum just a few hours ago. It felt like weeks—a year.

This morning, I'd been apprehensive, but still content and safe. Callum had seemed so strong, so confident and calm in the face of war.

But even Callum would have to admit how awful a day this had been. Watching a Witch's powers stolen from her, watching the life leave her body.

The Lightsmith, so unrepentant in his actions…

If you killed Merriwether, I swear, I'll rip your soul from your body. I will summon every monster in my imagination to tear you apart.

I felt like some part of me had been stolen today—some last shred of innocence that had clung desperately to my mind. My final, pathetic hope that the world was not as terrible as I feared…was gone.

I'd hoped to discover the Lightsmith was not a creature of pure cruelty—that even the most vicious monster could find a way to be merciful and kind.

But when I had looked into his cold eyes, devoid as they were of emotion, I had seen how lacking in kindness he really was. He reminded me of the Usurper Queen's awful husband Lumus, with his silver eyes and ice-cold demeanor.

They were like wretched twins separated at birth and sent to branch out and spread their awfulness throughout the land.

Right now, I wasn't sure which of them I hated more.

My legs shook when I closed my eyes and sent myself to the hallway just outside my grandfather's office in the Academy.

My hand trembled when I raised it to knock, weakened by fear just as my legs were.

"Merriwether?" I called, my voice a mere rasp.

There was no response.

I knocked again. "Grandfather!" I cried this time, terrified.

"You don't need to shout, dear girl."

The voice came from behind me.

I spun around and hurled myself into my grandfather's arms, squeezing him tight, as much to be sure he was really there as anything else.

"When I saw the road scorched like that…" I said, tears flowing freely now. "I thought…"

"You assumed the worst, naturally." He held me against him when he added, "Never forget, the Lightsmith deals in fear—a weapon more powerful than any other in his arsenal. But don't let him cast shadow and doubt over your mind, Granddaughter. He is to be pitied as *well* as feared."

"Pitied?" I asked, my brows meeting. "After what he did to Clio?"

Merriwether nodded. "The smith doesn't know right from wrong—at least, not exactly. He isn't like you or me. He is a creature of instinct alone. When he killed her, he was like a wild animal caught in a trap. He wants—*needs*—to survive, and for that reason, he doesn't take sides. His malice is a reflex—a means to an end, and that end is invariably self-preservation."

"But why did he have to be so cruel?" I asked. "And others, too. If it's not the Lightsmith coming for us, it's Waergs killing innocent people in their homes, or the queen terrorizing her subjects. Why can't the world just stop rewarding the most awful creatures and people in it?"

"You *know* why," Merriwether said softly. He pulled away to look me in the eye, wiping my tears from my cheeks as he did.

"Those who are kind-hearted tend to be kind to *everyone*—even to those who treat them badly. Which means the cruel take advantage of them. The truth is, most people don't ask for much. Most want only to live in peace, to enjoy quiet, happy existences. They long for a simple life—which is the basis of happiness, after all. True joy in life does not come from conquest, power, or money, contrary to popular belief. It comes from the small things. The scent of grass and leaves on a dewy morning. The sun, emerging from beyond a cloud before hiding itself again. A set of lovely eyes on an intelligent face. And there are still many of us in every world who value joy. The trouble is, those with hatred in their hearts tend to be the loudest. But make no mistake, Vega—we can and will silence them. For a time, at least."

I could feel the tears stinging my eyes again, and I tried hard to hold onto his words, to believe them.

Merriwether had lived far longer than I had. He had trained and fought long and hard over the years. He had suffered heartbreak. He understood better than anyone what it was to encounter foes so evil that they didn't think twice before stealing away a life...

Yet somehow, he was still whole. Still happy.

Or was he?

Lovely eyes on an intelligent face, he'd said. When he'd uttered those words, his voice had been wistful and filled with a longing I'd seldom heard from him.

Something told me he was speaking of my Nana—the woman he had loved so much so long ago. A woman who had given birth to their son, my father, only to raise him in another world, with another man.

I had a strong suspicion that Merriwether *still* loved her—and that she still loved him.

It broke my heart that they couldn't be together now. After all, the man Nana had married—the man I'd called Grandfather for years—had died.

Which meant my Nana was alone.

Part of me wondered if they would—if they *could*—ever find their way back to one another. In their youth, such a union had proved impossible. The scandal was too great for my grandmother to stay in the Otherwhere, and Merriwether aged too rapidly in our world to live there with her.

Maybe in the end, they could find their way back to one another.

But that was a dream for another day.

18
PRISON

"Where is the Lightsmith?" I asked Merriwether, dragging myself back to the present. "Did you...?"

"Kill him?"

He shook his head and slipped his hands behind his back, sighing.

"No, I didn't."

"Why not?" I blurted out, my voice more aggressive than I intended. "He murdered a Witch! He would have killed Solara, too, or me, or—"

Merriwether held a hand up to silence me. "Because, my dear, the Orb has told me he has an important role to play in the coming days."

"But I thought..."

"You thought I wanted him dead." My grandfather nodded solemnly. "Truth be told, so did I. I was certain of it, in fact. But you must trust me now. Trust the Orb of Kilarin. Let us mourn the Witch who died, and tread carefully. This matter isn't so simple as it seems."

"It *is* simple," I said, my jaw clenched, "The Lightsmith is our enemy."

Merriwether looked pained when he replied, "You may as well say arrows are the enemy, or a blade that lies on the ground is the enemy. The Lightsmith is, at his core, a weapon of sorts. That makes him dangerous. But when wielded by the right hands, he may prove a valuable asset."

"I don't see how. The creature I saw on that road can't be controlled. You said yourself that he's like an animal going on instinct." My chest was tight when I added, "Isn't he?"

"He's not currently a threat to our lives, if that's what you mean. I have imprisoned him in a special cell here in the Academy. He didn't hurt me—I suspect he knew I would not kill him, which meant he had no reason to take my life. I managed to transport him to our dungeon single-handedly and without doing him too much harm."

I narrowed my eyes, confused. I'd seen the massive crater of black in the road. If Merriwether was unharmed and if the Lightsmith was, too, then I wasn't sure I wanted to know what had happened to wreak so much havoc.

"I said without *too much* harm," Merriwether said, reading my expression. "I did fire off a warning shot or two to subdue him—which is why the road was destroyed. So yes, I suppose you might say the smith can be controlled, at least a little. Perhaps it will be enough, in the end. And when all this is over—when we have uncovered the treasure from the prophecy and set the true heir on the throne—we can all rest, at least for a time." With a hard exhalation, he added, "I, for one, am due for a holiday."

"The *treasure*," I repeated. "I'd almost forgotten the prophecy mentioned it. Do you have any thoughts on what it is? Is it something Callum is supposed to search for?"

Merriwether shook his head, doleful. "Your guess is as good as mine, I'm afraid. I'd love to tell you there's a buried chest under an enormous X at the Otherwhere's center, but we both know prophecies aren't so simple as all that. Still, if anyone can find it, it's Callum. With our help, of course."

My heartbeat accelerated then, a sudden urge overtaking me to see Callum. "Where *is* he? Do you know?"

I was agitated, worried—terrified, even, that he had been through an ordeal even worse than ours. If he'd been to the mountains, it was entirely possible he'd been confronted by Waergs, Ursals, or worse.

"He's still with Caffall," Merriwether said confidently, putting my mind at ease. "I have no doubt they'll be home before long. In the meantime, you should go somewhere and relax. Today may be the last time you get a chance to do so for a while."

Something in his tone told me that as usual, he knew more than he was letting on.

"Stop worrying about me, Granddaughter," he chuckled. "I'm fine, as you can see. But I need to think and strategize, and in the meantime, the last thing I want is for you to worry about Callum, me, or anyone else. You have your own trials and tribulations to worry about. Your body and mind will be tested in the very near future, I'm afraid, and you will learn what it is to be a fighter. So go and do something that brings you joy. It's the most important thing in life, and there's little chance of it during times of war."

"It's not the worst idea in the world," I said, a spontaneous desire entering my mind. "I think I'll go to Fairhaven for a little. I want…I *need*…"

Merriwether smiled, understanding what I was trying and failing to say. "You want something comforting and familiar. Something far from this chaotic place. I can't say I blame you. Go, then. Come back when you're ready—nothing will change here in the meantime, I assure you."

Turning to walk away, I replied, "I'll be back soon. If Callum returns, tell him where I am, would you?"

"Of course I will. And Vega…"

I twisted to face him. "Yes?"

"Thank you for checking in on me. I appreciate it more than you know."

With that, he disappeared into his office.

19
HOME

I found myself standing at the front door of Liv's family home.

My heart calmed as I inhaled Fairhaven's familiar air. My body relaxed for the first time in what felt like an eternity, my shoulders dropping, my breathing slowing.

I was home.

Only…it didn't entirely feel like home.

Not anymore.

It was more like an escape from the reality I was now a part of. A momentary lapse in what had become a danger-filled life.

Summer had hit Fairhaven, and the air was stifling. It was the kind of heat that made me want to seek out a pretty tree and take a nap in its shade, for lack of energy to do anything else.

At least I was far from the Lightsmith and the Usurper Queen.

But I was also far from Callum, Merriwether, and everything else I loved so much about the Otherwhere.

To say my emotions were mixed would have been a huge understatement.

I took a deep breath, savoring the calming feeling of

normality that came from being in Fairhaven again, and knocked on the door.

A few seconds later, Liv pulled it open, a beaming smile alighting on her face.

"Vega!" she cried and drew me into a bear hug. "I knew it would be you!"

I managed a laugh then pulled back to ask, "How could you possibly have known that?"

"No idea," she said with a shrug. "I just felt it. Like—I was worried you were in danger or something?"

I stared at her, my eyes wide.

"I know, I know," she sighed. "It's stupid."

"No, it's not. I *was* in danger. I mean, sort of. I—"

But I found I couldn't get the words out, not without telling her what had happened. What I'd seen. A Witch, dead. A powerful magic user, her life stolen in front of my eyes. I'd failed to help her, to protect her. I'd just watched as her life had been stolen away.

Liv knew about the Otherwhere and about Merriwether and Callum. She knew dragons and magic were as real as the grass on her front lawn.

But I still couldn't bear to subject her to my sadness.

"Let's go for a walk," she said cheerfully, seeming to sense what I needed. She ushered me away from the door so she could pull it shut behind us. "I've already got my shoes on. May as well get some exercise, right?"

"I'm not taking you from your parents?"

"Nah. They won't even notice I'm gone. They're obsessively bingeing some Netflix series upstairs. Probably one of their murder shows." With a roll of her eyes, she added, "They love their murder."

When we came to the sidewalk, Liv leaned in close as if she sensed I needed support. "Tell me, what happened?" she asked in a near-whisper—a vocal level that was highly unusual for her.

"Do you really want to know?" I asked. "It's…a lot."

She jabbed me in the arm. "Of course I want to know. How am I supposed to help my bestie feel better if I have no idea what's making her look like the weight of the world is crouching like a gargoyle on her shoulders?"

I hesitated, sighed, then proceeded to tell her everything—about the Lightsmith and what he could do. About Lachlan, Lily, the Witches—and what had happened on the road. About my grandfather finally ensnaring the Lightsmith, who was now trapped between the Academy's walls.

Liv took it all in stride, like she was now entirely accustomed to hearing about the bizarre happenings of a magical world separate from our own.

"Do you feel safe with him there?" she asked. "I mean, I know Merriwether is powerful and all that, but this Lightsmith dude sounds…I don't know, unhinged?"

"I'm not sure about safe," I admitted, my eyes moving to a bird flitting overhead. "But I don't think he's there to kill any of us. The truth is, I don't think he would have killed that Witch if she hadn't gone after him. He was headed to the Academy because he wants to destroy the Relics—which is almost worse than wanting to hurt us. If he does that…if he escapes his cell and gets hold of them…"

"Wait—he wants to destroy the Relics? That's all?" Liv asked with a dismissive wave of her hand.

I stopped walking and took her by the arm, halting her. "Liv, the Relics are the whole reason I trained with the other Seekers. One of us died. We fought tooth and nail—literally—to bring them to the Academy and keep them out of the Usurper Queen's hands."

"Well, sure," Liv said. "I get it. But isn't destroying them another way to keep them out of her hands?"

"What do you mean?" I retorted, baffled. "They're what gives us our power. The Academy—Merriwether, Callum...we all benefit from them. They're important."

"Pfft," Liv scoffed. "No, they're not. Come on—do you really think some lyre or scepter is why you're all so powerful? Do you think some trinkets are going to change the course of the Otherwhere's future?"

She seemed so confident, so assured that I waited for her to continue. The truth was, I didn't know what to say in response.

"Look," she said, "I'm no Witch or Wizard or anything, but it seems to me your gramps was pretty damned powerful *before* he had his hands on the Relics of Power, and so was Callum—and for that matter, so were you. Seriously, 'Relics of Power' is a dumb name that makes everyone think they're something more than they are. It implies you need them in order to be strong."

When I stared, stunned into silence, she laughed and said, "Vega—don't you get it yet?"

"Get what?"

"Maybe the Relics are just *symbols*. Maybe the real power lies with all of you. You're all hiding behind a bunch of ancient objects, but they can't fight *for* you. You have to do that yourselves."

I shook my head. "There has to be more to them than just symbolism." But even as I spoke, I wasn't sure. "Doesn't there?"

"I honestly don't know." Liv let out a hefty sigh. "All I'm saying is, if something happens to them, don't tell yourself all is lost. As long as you, Callum, Merriwether, and that hottie Lachlan are still around, you'll be fine. I know it."

Maybe Liv was right. Maybe the Relics didn't give us our strength, so much as *convince* us we were strong.

Maybe they had already rendered us as powerful as we were ever going to be, simply by bringing us all together.

Since when is Liv the wise one? I thought with a snicker.

20
B.F.F.

"If the Relics don't give us our strength," I said to Liv, "why does Merriwether need to hold onto the Lightsmith? Why not just give him the Relics to destroy, or destroy them himself?"

"Why does Merriwether do anything?" Liv laughed with a shrug. "No offense, but that guy is a little loopy, you have to admit. I mean, he's great and all—but he's also certifiably bananas."

"He's a *Wizard*," I snapped.

"Exactly."

At that, I finally managed a proper, hearty laugh. I threw an arm around Liv, grateful that she always managed to put a positive spin on the most terrible and terrifying situations, and we kept walking toward Fairhaven's downtown.

"I'm so glad I came home for a little," I told her. "I needed you more than I knew."

"I'm glad to know I'm still needed, Vega," she replied with a chuckle. "Sometimes I worry I'll lose you to the Otherwhere forever."

I grinned, but I didn't answer. The truth was, she might lose me yet—but I would do everything in my power to make sure our bond never broke. Even though I hadn't entirely committed to one future or the other, I had no intention of deserting Liv or Will.

"So," she said, "do you want to go to Perks with me for an iced mocha monstrosity, for old times' sake?"

"Sure," I sighed. "But then I need to head back. I'm worried about Callum, after everything that happened today. The Otherwhere's getting to be such a dangerous—"

"Place," a deep voice said from behind us. "But you don't need to worry about me, Sloane."

Stopping abruptly, I twisted around to see Callum standing a few feet away.

I leapt into his arms, kissing him as gratitude overwhelmed me—both to find he was okay, and for the fact that he'd known I wouldn't be able to relax until I knew he was all right.

"Good grief," Liv said with a roll of her eyes. "You two are so adorable it makes me want to puke."

I smiled, pulling back, then drew my eyes curiously to the clear sky above us.

"Caffall?" I asked as Callum pressed a soft kiss to my forehead. "Where is he?"

"He's back in the Otherwhere," he replied. "We're trying a little something—out of curiosity. I wanted to see if I could come here without inflicting pain on either of us—you know, for future reference."

"Really? And you're both…okay with that? I mean, it's not hurting you or him?"

He nodded. "Oh, it definitely hurts. Still, I suspect we can call it a success."

"It hurts, but it's a success?" Liv asked. "Has anyone ever pointed out you're a masochist, Drake?"

"Maybe I am," Callum admitted with a snicker. "Caffall is part of me. The golden dragon and I have a strong bond. I can feel him, even from this world. Which is how I know we're okay."

Liv wrapped an arm around mine and said, "You know, it would hurt if Vega and I were torn apart, too. So for the record, if you take her away from me forever, you have to grant me visitation rights. I want to make that clear right now."

Callum laughed. "I wouldn't dare argue with you, Liv. I promise—you will get to see her as often as you like..." He glanced at me. "*If* she chooses to stay in the Otherwhere."

"You're really okay, Callum?" I said, changing the subject and looking around before adding, "Did you find anything out from the Grells?"

"I met with Kohrin to talk strategy, and I learned something about the queen's troop movements. But my day was far less eventful than yours, Vega." His face dropped when he added, "I'm so sorry about what happened to Clio."

I nodded. "Me, too," I said, sadness driving its way through me. "I guess you know Merriwether has the Lightsmith?"

With a solemn nod, he said, "I do."

"Do you think he'll be safe in the Academy?"

"I think *we'll* be safe, and that's what matters. Your grandfather—well, he may not show off, but he's the best spell-caster around. If he wants the smith in a cell, then in a cell is where he'll stay."

"Look, do you two want to go to Perks or not?" Liv asked, crossing her arms impatiently. "Because I need an iced mocha right now. All this talk of enemies is making me thirsty."

"Sorry, Liv," I said, and we all began walking again. "We'll get you your chocolatey abomination. But I'm sure Callum will need to head home soon, and so will I."

"Home," she repeated, sighing a little. "Do you even realize what you just said? That the Otherwhere is your home, and not Fairhaven?"

"I'm well aware," I replied, kicking myself a little. "I guess I have two homes."

She stared at me for a moment, then turned back to the sidewalk, shrugged, and said, "I guess that's okay. I'm moving to Boston next year, anyhow. Even if you stayed here, I'd never see you."

"Liv—what?" I squeaked. "Seriously?"

"Seriously. I'm going to get a job for the year, then head to university when I've figured out what the hell I want to do with my life. Right now, it's totally up in the air."

"Speaking of things that are up in the air," Callum said sheepishly, "I do need to get back to Caffall. I'll see you tonight—but take all the time you need."

I was about to say goodbye when I asked, "How did you get here?"

When Callum lowered his chin and shot me a look, I laughed. "One of Merriwether's portals," I said. "Of course."

"He's the greatest asset and ally I can imagine. I don't know what we'll do if he ever chooses to leave the Academy."

"I can't even imagine," I agreed. "But let's not worry about that just now. You have a much more important fate to contend with."

Callum hugged me tight, whispering into my ear. "Come back to me safely. But don't rush."

"There's a war raging," I said. "I don't really have a choice."

"The war isn't at the Academy's gates quite yet. And if we play our cards right, it will never make it that far. Now, you relax for a bit. Remember what you're fighting for—what we're *all* fighting for—and come back when you're ready."

I nodded, holding back tears as we said goodbye.

Callum's words held more meaning than Liv knew—than anyone in my world knew.

I would never have said it out loud, but if things went badly in the Otherwhere, the Usurper Queen would retaliate by attacking my world. The Waergs under her command would do her bidding, regardless of how vile and gruesome her demands might be.

We would have to stop her at any cost. It was the only conceivable solution.

"I'll see you soon," I said, kissing Callum one last time before he headed toward the Novel Hovel, where I knew Merriwether's temporary portal must be awaiting him.

21
INTRUDERS

When we'd purchased a mocha with extra chocolate for Liv and an iced latte for me, we headed across the street to the Fairhaven Commons, the large park where we'd spent so many hours in our youth.

It was green, lush, and crisscrossed with paths to walk or bike along, many of them lined with comfortable park benches. Half of Fairhaven's population was out today either playing frisbee, lying in the sun, or enjoying a picnic in the shade.

The setting felt beautifully normal, and for a calm moment, I managed to forget all that the Witches, Lachlan, and I had endured back in the Otherwhere.

Liv and I took a seat on a bench in the shade of an oak tree and let out a synchronized sigh as we slouched back.

"How glad are you not to be returning to Plymouth High in the fall?" she asked.

"Are you joking?" I snickered. "I was ready to leave that place three years ago, and I'd be perfectly happy never to see it again. High school is hot garbage."

Liv let out a laugh. "Tell me how you *really* feel, Vega."

We chattered on for a few minutes about our hatred of the

teenage experience, blissful to soak in the summer warmth until something in the distance caught my eye, setting me instantly on edge.

Moving down the paved path toward us at a rapid pace was a tall-ish young woman with freshly dyed waves of platinum blond hair.

The hair wasn't surprising. What *was* surprising was that she looked like she couldn't wait to get close to us.

As many times as I'd seen Miranda Smythe in my life, I couldn't say I'd ever seen her look eager to see Liv or me.

"Well, if it isn't the Queen of the Charmers," I muttered under my breath.

The Charmers were the trio of "popular" girls who had tormented Liv and me for years. There was a time not so long ago when I would have winced to see Miranda heading toward us. But now, empowered as I was, I knew perfectly well that if anyone in this scenario should be afraid, it was her.

"Ugh, what's *she* doing here?" Liv asked, then mimed dry-heaving.

At first, I wondered the same thing. But when Miranda peered over her shoulder and I spied a figure behind her—a young man with fire in his eyes and a snarl on his lips—I understood.

"That's a Waerg," I said under my breath, pushing myself to my feet before muttering, "Why would a Waerg be after her, of all people?"

"What?" Liv snapped, leaping up to stand beside me, her stance almost comically combative as if she could take him in a fight. Even *I* couldn't—not without some major help from my small arsenal of spells.

"Vega! Olivia! Thank God you're both here," Miranda huffed, her tone exasperated. She held up a small pink shopping bag. "I was just buying a new skirt and that guy—" She glanced over her shoulder, then shuddered. "He asked if I knew you, Vega. I asked why he cared, then walked away. You know—Street Smarts and all that—and ever since, he's been, well, *following* me." She sounded proud of this, as if it was an honor to be stalked by a strange man. Leaning in close, she whispered, "Do you know who he is? I mean, he's hot and everything, but he doesn't exactly seem friendly."

I stared at the young man who had now stopped following her and stood some distance from us, his arms crossed, chin down like a surly child. I didn't recognize the Waerg—I had no idea if he was part of Lachlan's former pack or another.

Not that it mattered.

Any Waerg in Fairhaven was a potential threat.

"Get behind me, Miranda," I said, ignoring her questions. My high school nemesis glared at me as if she was affronted that I would dare issue her an order. "Get behind me, or I may just let him kill you."

With that, her expression altered to one of pure fear. Liv grabbed her arm and pulled her behind me just in time for me to step forward to confront the Waerg.

"Who the hell are you?" I snarled, striding toward him.

"Vega Sloane," he replied, ignoring the question. "Fancy meeting you here. We were afraid you were in the Otherwhere."

"The *what*?" Miranda asked.

"Shut up!" Liv hissed. "Honestly, Miranda, if you don't stop talking, I'm going to cut your hair off with my teeth."

"What do you want?" I asked the Waerg, crossing my arms.

He glanced at my left hand to see the ring Callum had given me, and for a moment he looked shocked, even disoriented.

"Where did you get that?"

"I asked you a question," I retorted, tucking my hand under my arm to conceal the ring. "What do you want? And why were you after Miranda?"

"I wanted to find you," he replied. "Isn't it obvious?"

"And you thought *Miranda* would be a good resource for that sort of information?"

He shrugged, issuing me an annoying smirk. "I've seen you two speaking before. I assumed you were friends."

I laughed. I couldn't help it.

"Miranda is hardly my friend," I managed between chuckles. "Still—she's human. And if you touch her, I *will* find you and kill you."

"You're nothing but a Seeker," he scoffed. "You're no magical warrior."

After what I'd been through, confronting this irritating gnat of a Waerg was beginning to feel almost comical. I had no fear of him—in fact, I was beginning to sense he feared me, despite his arrogant façade.

Even my ring had frightened him, though I had no idea why.

"I'm a Seeker, a Shadow, and a Summoner." I raised a hand into the air to call forth a creature of flame—a warrior—who appeared between the Waerg and me. As I commanded him silently, the conjured warrior held a fiery hand up in the air. A flaming sword appeared, its hilt grasped firmly in his fist.

He stepped toward the Waerg who hunched in submission, an animalistic whine escaping his lips.

I could hear Miranda muttering something behind me, terrified.

By now, others in the park had begun to stare, too, and I murmured an incantation, stopping time and freezing all of them before they could pull out their cell phones and record what was happening.

Everyone, that was, but the Waerg, Liv, and me.

I would have to make the onlookers forget later—but for now, I had more important business to attend to.

"The Mistress wants a meeting," the Waerg said, drawing his eyes back to mine. "She sent an envoy to instruct us that if we found you, we were to secure a meeting in any way we could."

"And you figured you'd threaten a human girl to get what you wanted?" I didn't bother asking how the Usurper Queen's envoy had reached my world. Lumus, her husband, was powerful—and this was no doubt his doing.

"I suppose I got lucky finding you here," the man said, "You know, if a certain Waerg in the Otherwhere were behaving himself, he could have informed you himself of the Mistress's wishes. But I hear he's been hanging out with Witches like some common traitor."

At that, my blood boiled and froze at once. "Lachlan is no Waerg," I scowled. "He's far more powerful than your ilk. Besides, you should be so lucky as to live in the company of Witches."

He laughed. "Lachlan is a fool, and one day soon, he'll suffer the consequences of his actions. But no matter. It's *you* the queen wants to see. Will you go to her?"

"When?"

"At your earliest convenience, of course," he said, eyeing Miranda over my shoulder. "If you don't, I can't say your pal here will remain safe."

"You wouldn't dare hurt her," I said, deliberately neglecting to mention that Liv was a far better friend to me than Miranda could ever be.

"Why do you care? You said yourself that you're not close."

At my silent command, the flame-warrior stepped closer to the Waerg, who gnashed a set of jagged teeth at him and let out a low growl.

"Fire doesn't fear your fangs," I said. "As for why I care—I told you, Miranda is a human who lives in this peaceful town, and this isn't *her* war. Just as it's not the war of the many innocent humans in the Otherwhere who are being killed by your beloved Mistress's forces. Still, I will meet with your so-called queen. I'll hear what she has to say, if it saves just one life."

"How noble of you," the Waerg replied, disdain painting his words.

I'd had just about enough of the bastard's attitude.

At my command, the flame-warrior raised his sword high and moved to strike.

The Waerg shifted into his wolf form, turned tail, and fled as fast as his four legs would carry him.

22

FAREWELL TO FAIRHAVEN

WITH A FLICK OF MY FINGERS, THE FLAME-WARRIOR DISAPPEARED AS if he'd never been there.

Turning to face Liv, I saw that she wasn't moving. Her eyes stared, unblinking, into the distance.

"I didn't freeze you," I said, and she shook her head, the whites of her eyes prominent.

"No, you didn't," she replied, loosening her shoulders and relaxing. "I just didn't want wolf-boy to know we're friends. I can't believe they thought Miranda was your bestie. Those Waergs aren't the sharpest tools in the shed, are they?"

"Maybe they avoided coming for you because they know you and Lachlan were close," I laughed. "Something tells me they're a little afraid of what he might do to them—especially knowing Meligant is his father."

"Good. They *should* be afraid." Liv let out a shudder.

"Are you okay?"

"Fine. I mean, I'll never quite get used to that whole..." She waved a hand at the space around us. "Magic and mayhem thing. But at least around you, I feel safe."

I let out a chuckle as I grabbed Miranda's and Liv's hands,

then cast the spell to make everyone else in the park forget they'd seen a creature of flame.

When that was done, I cast another spell to unfreeze time.

"What *was* that thing?" Miranda whispered, collapsing onto the bench as if her legs had given out. Her voice was high-pitched and frantic. Sweat beaded on her forehead, and I could tell she was on the verge of going into shock—just as I'd been the first time I encountered a Waerg.

Recalling a bit of magic I'd once seen Solara use on a panicking mortal, I passed a hand through the air, casting a calming spell. Whatever Liv and I said in the next few minutes would seem perfectly rational and reasonable to her, regardless of how unfathomable it might be to most of Fairhaven's human population.

"It was a Waerg," Liv said, like it was the most common of knowledge. "A human who can shift into a wolf."

"No," Miranda replied, her voice softer now. "I didn't mean the guy. I meant the fire-thingie."

At that, I laughed. "He was just a little something I conjured with my mind. No biggie."

Miranda's eyes went wide, then narrowed. For a split-second, she *almost* looked like she admired me.

Almost.

"I always knew you were a freak," she finally said. But instead of the usual disgust in her voice, I thought I detected the faintest hint of admiration.

"You're welcome," I told her. "Look—I could have made you forget you saw anything, but he threatened you. I need you and the other Charmers to stay on your toes, all right? For some reason, the Waerg is convinced we're pals."

Miranda winced. "Fine. And while we're talking, maybe you could move on from calling us *Charmers*."

There are far worse things that I could call you, Miranda.

I rolled my eyes. "Just...keep an eye on your friends. If

anything weird starts happening, find Liv and tell her right away. Okay?"

Miranda nodded.

Liv sat down next to her and elbowed her in the ribs. "You do know Vega just saved your ass, right?"

"I guess. I mean, it's not like that Wae—whatever you call him—actually did anything to me."

"That guy would never have left you alone if it weren't for Vega. She's made sure he won't stalk you."

Miranda shrugged. "Maybe I wanted to be stalked. He really was pretty cute."

"You have terrible taste in men, Miranda," I muttered.

"Hey—I had a major crush on your Callum for a while," she protested, pouting.

Our eyes met, and for the first time in our lives, we shared a genuine laugh.

"Fine," I said. "But do yourself a favor and don't date a Waerg. And if you see one of them again, tell them you're under my protection."

Miranda rolled her eyes. "Seriously? Do I *have* to say that?"

"Well, you could keep quiet, and they might just eat your face," Liv sneered. "It's your choice."

"Ugh," Miranda replied. "Fine. What do I owe you for it? Do you want me to keep all this a secret?"

Liv laughed. "You don't have to keep it secret. But trust me—if you tell people, they'll look at you like you have three heads."

"You have a point there."

"Look, Miranda," I said. "Just try to be nicer to people. Not everyone is out to ruin your life, you know. You were horrible to Liv and me all through high school. We've had enough."

"That was only because—" Miranda began, but she stopped herself.

"Because…?" I asked.

"Because you two were so—I don't know, *happy*. I couldn't stand it."

I could have chewed her out for going after us for such a petty reason. But instead, I asked, "You really thought I was happy? My parents were killed when I needed them most. I was *far* from happy!"

"I know that," Miranda said. "Of course I do. And everyone sympathized and felt bad for you, and they were all so nice to you." Her face flushed with shame as she made the confession. "It still upset me. Look, I may have parents, Vega—but they may as well be dead. I was raised by a rotating crew of nannies. I was never close to any of them, but I was even less close to my mother and father. I don't think my parents have ever cared that I existed. At least you had parents who loved you—and you had your brother, Will. I never had anyone."

I was stunned.

I couldn't believe this girl—this beautiful girl who had long been the envy of everyone, including me, for so long—was seriously standing before me and insisting that I was somehow fortunate to have lost my parents.

Yet there was some part of me that understood what she was saying, and how hard it must have been for her to admit this weakness on her part.

"I'm sorry," I said, swallowing the desire to argue. "That must suck."

"It does. But I..." She glanced at Liv, then me, then inhaled a deep breath, like she was preparing herself for a sacrifice. "I'm sorry, too. I was an ass to you both, and you didn't deserve it. I just needed to take out my hurt on someone, you know?"

Liv and I shot each other a quick side-eye, silently asking, "Is she for real?"

In the end, it was Liv who said, "We forgive you, Miranda," then, as if to get away from the cringe-worthy subject, added, "Hey—are you going to university in the fall?"

"I am," Miranda replied. "Boston University!" A broad smile broke out over her lips as she and Liv turned toward home.

"What? I'll be there, too!" Liv said, bouncing up and down, all the years of Miranda's torment forgotten. "I mean, not at the school—but in Beantown."

"Liv!" I called out, and she turned around to focus her eyes on me. "I have to go back. They need me."

My heart hurt to unleash the words. As much as I wanted to be back in Callum's arms and near my grandfather, to watch over the place and the people I loved so much—the thought of leaving Fairhaven for what might be the last time?

It stung.

Something told me if I ever saw my hometown again, I would be seeing it through the eyes of someone profoundly changed.

Liv leapt at me, hugged me tight, and whispered, "Good luck —and remember what I told you. The Relics may be important, but they mean nothing in the end. It's *all you*." She pulled back and added, "And if you need help, you know where to find me. I may not know how to wield a sword or cast a spell or do anything useful. But I'm *amazing* at moral support."

At that, I laughed, gave her one last hug, then watched her and Miranda—the most unlikely pair in the history of the universe— walk away from me.

It was time to me to leave Fairhaven, and I wouldn't be back until the war was over.

I shuddered as I found myself wondering if I'd ever be back at all.

23
THE MISTRESS

I should have headed straight back to the safety of the Academy.

Time passed differently in our two worlds, but if I didn't head back soon, Callum and Merriwether would begin to feel my absence—and they'd definitely worry about me. But I couldn't seem to dislodge the Waerg's words from my mind:

"The Mistress wants a meeting."

My fate—my whole life, in fact—had been tied to the Academy for what felt like ages now. I was bound to Callum and to my grandfather. I had helped find and bring the Relics to the Academy. The Lightsmith was now a captive.

I supposed we were as prepared to do battle as we'd ever be.

But...what if we could avoid an outright battle? If the Usurper Queen wanted a meeting, then maybe she was willing to negotiate. I was Merriwether's granddaughter and Callum's unofficial fiancée, after all. Maybe she saw me as a potential negotiator—someone who could listen to her demands or whatever she wanted to throw my way and bring them to the Academy.

"Who the hell am I kidding?" I muttered with a snicker. The Usurper Queen was hardly the sort of person to negotiate. She would burn the world to the ground before choosing to be reasonable.

Still, why would she want me in her presence? I wasn't the one who was meant to sit on the throne.

With a cynical sneer, I told myself I knew the answer. The queen probably wanted to trap me—to hold me hostage and demand that Callum and Merriwether back down.

Which meant I had to make sure she and Lumus didn't outwit me.

In their own castle, that would be more easily said than done.

I TRANSPORTED myself to the gates of Uldrach, the grim structure that stood in the midst of the fallen city of Kaer Uther.

The castle itself was the domain of three of my greatest enemies: the Usurper Queen, Lumus, and their son, Raff—a boy I trusted even less than I would a venomous snake. When we'd first met, I had foolishly thought him a friend. But as it turned out, he had deceived me into trusting him.

In the end, I'd come to despise him almost as much as I hated his atrocious parents.

I hadn't seen Raff in ages—not since the battle for the Sword of Viviane—and had no desire to see him now.

I stood at the castle gates, knowing full well that I could simply have brought myself to the throne room. I'd been there before, after all. I knew the space all too well.

But transporting myself directly to the castle's center might be interpreted as a threat, and I wanted to do this the right way. I was a guest. An intermediary.

I turned and for a moment I took in the derelict town of Kaer Uther, its ruined façades mere shadows of their former glory. The entire place looked like a burnt-out husk, the soulless remains of a once-beautiful city.

As I stared out, my chest tight with rage, Uldrach's gates creaked open behind me, drawing me into the palace grounds.

With a sigh I turned again and stepped through, peering around cautiously as Waerg guards patrolled the inner courtyard. Some were in their wolf forms, others in leather or silver armor. Every single one of them eyed me with a hunger that told me they wanted to dig their claws and fangs into me—and would have, if not for the hold their queen had over them.

I'd just begun to stride toward the portcullis across the courtyard when a figure moved toward me—a tall man with long legs and dark hair.

"Vega Sloane," he said, his voice smooth, his brows meeting in judgment. It was as though he knew me by reputation but expected me to be far more daunting.

"Yes," I replied, stopping, my body tightening. "And you are...?"

"Julyan, butler to Queen Isla, Mistress of the Otherwhere," he replied with a bow of his head. "At your service."

"I doubt that."

He pulled his head up, his eyes flashing with a revelation of his inner beast, and turned on his heel, a gray cloak swirling around him. "Come, the queen awaits you."

I followed him in surly silence, recalling my unpleasant memories of this place. This castle was rightfully Callum's—but it was a castle I couldn't imagine inhabiting. Something about it was so foreboding and so deliberately grim that I couldn't even begin to see its appeal. Even in the right hands, it would always have a cold, prison-like quality.

I couldn't imagine someone as good as Callum making it a home. And whether I wanted to admit it to myself or not, I didn't ever want to live under its roof.

My happiest memories with Callum had formed under open skies with sun and clouds and fresh air surrounding us both. They were simple, beautiful times that I would never willingly surrender, especially not in exchange for the dark arches and ornate stonework of Uldrach Castle.

Then again, much of Uldrach's depressing appearance was a consequence of the queen and her husband. They had reveled in its downfall, just as they had reveled in the destruction of their realm.

The city of Kaer Uther had once been beautiful and might be again one day, if Callum took the throne. For now, though, I couldn't begin to contemplate that ideal future. All I cared about was confronting the queen for the atrocities her forces had committed.

Callum and Merriwether would not be happy with me when they heard I'd come to this place—but I knew perfectly well I could hold my own against Isla. I'd done it before.

Besides, surely, she hadn't summoned me to her home in order to murder me. Had she?

I followed Julyan until we reached the all-too familiar Throne Room. Without the Waerg guards, the lit braziers and the caged dragons, the chamber seemed even larger than ever before—but thankfully, it also felt less daunting.

The massive, stone-walled chamber looked almost sad now, a lonely, echoing place devoid of an ounce of warmth—unlike the Great Hall at the Academy.

Julyan escorted me up to the throne, then bowed his head and left me standing there while I glanced around, my mind keenly focused on the fact that I might need to make a rapid escape before too long if Lumus or his wife tried anything stupid.

"Vega, Daughter of Viviane," a familiar, nausea-inspiring voice called out, echoing like the tips of daggers off the chamber walls.

I turned to see the queen stalking out from a side door with Lumus in his silver wolf form right behind her.

The queen's light brown hair was twisted into a series of elegant braids on top of her head, her lips painted crimson.

As they padded along, the wolf shifted, but Lumus's silver eyes stayed locked on me.

"I'm here. What do you want?" I snarled, refusing to call Isla *Highness* or *Queen*.

She looked injured by my curt tone, like my rudeness was crueler than the many murders her forces had committed in recent days.

"Is that any way to speak to your future sister-in-law?" she asked.

Admittedly, I was taken aback by the question. But when I saw her staring down at my ring, I understood.

"That was my brother's doing, was it not?" she asked. "That ring is deeply familiar to me, you know. They say it once belonged to another queen—so if you ask me, it should have come to me."

I played with the ring for a moment. So, it was an heirloom, was it?

I made a mental note to ask Callum about it...if I ever got out of Uldrach alive.

"Yes, your brother gave it to me," I snapped, feeling the power of the amplifier stone embedded in the silver. A stone that had once been inlaid in a certain dragon key. "But whatever happens, I will never call you sister, Isla. Not for anything."

"Pity," she cooed, her red lips pouting slightly.

"Why did you ask me to come here? And why the hell are your Waergs stalking humans in Fairhaven?"

At that, her lips turned up in a smile. "I'm sure you can guess, Vega dear. I want you and yours to know your world is not safe. If you do not leave me to my throne—if you don't return to your home and leave the Otherwhere behind—then there will be trouble. Even now, my army is moving toward the Academy for the Blood-Born, and I suspect you know what *that* means."

The words and the thought of that were equally horrific.

I had seen the repercussions of Isla's Ursals tearing the countryside apart. I knew perfectly well what they were capable of.

But there was no way in hell I was going to admit how frightened I felt of what her minions could do. Instead, I let out a laugh.

"You stole the throne—and now you intend to keep it by threatening humans in my world?"

"You've seen what I can do. You shouldn't doubt me."

I narrowed my eyes at her, then pulled my gaze to Lumus.

"Tell me," I said, "Do you enjoy it when your wife goes into full psycho mode?"

Lumus raised his chin, attempting to stare me down. The first time I met him, the intimidation tactic had worked. He *was* a warlock, after all...and a powerful one.

But I had power, too.

And the ring on my finger served to amplify it.

"I will support the queen in whatever she decides to do," he said. "If she wishes to burn the Otherwere to the ground, I am here for it."

"And let me guess—you'd love it, wouldn't you?" I asked bitterly. "Of course you would. You're a monster, just like her."

Turning back to Isla, I said, "You're scared. That's why you want me gone. You're afraid of what I can do. Afraid of what Callum and Caffall are capable of."

"Ridiculous," she retorted. "Lumus here is stronger than you'll ever be."

"What about you?" I asked. "You, who hide behind an army of beasts? Are you strong, Isla, or is it fear that drives you?" I took a step toward her and watched as she recoiled before regaining her composure and lifting her chin.

"You don't know what you're talking about," she snapped.

Not for the first time, she was reminding me of Miranda—someone who projected strength and confidence, but at her core was frightened that the world would discover her weakness.

"Your Waergs and Ursals have killed many innocent people," I said. "Too many. It's time to stop. You know by now that we have the Lightsmith in custody. The Relics are still ours. You can't possibly win."

"Oh—we will win," she said. "But I promise you, I'll spare your precious Academy—I will call off my dogs. But only if you convince Callum to give up his quest for the throne. Promise that you'll bring him to your world to live, and I will stop the war here and now."

24

A TRUCE

At that, I froze.

I did *not* expect those words from her.

The Usurper Queen was really offering a truce. *An actual truce.* Lives could be saved.

But the price she was demanding was far too high.

"I can't do that," I said softly, my gaze falling to the floor. "I can't ask Callum to surrender his birthright. He's suffered for countless years because of what your family did to him. You stole his life away—you and your parents. It's time to make things right and to give the Otherwhere their true leader."

Her voice bit through the air when she spoke again. "Come, now. Callum doesn't even want to be king. He never has. It's you and that damned prophecy that have made him think it's his fate. That stupid boy has always had far too strong a sense of duty."

"Callum wants what's best for the Otherwhere," I replied, shaking my head and struggling to keep my voice level. "And everyone in these lands knows you are not the leader they need. The prophecy says the rightful heir will take the throne—*that* is what the Otherwhere desires."

"The prophecy also says the so-called 'rightful heir' might just burn the lands to the ground. Perhaps it's time to admit prophecies are not worth the paper they're scrawled on."

"He won't burn anything," I snarled. "He wouldn't. You know it as well as I do. Callum is good and kind. He's not like you."

Isla threw her head back and laughed. "My brother would have my head on a spike if he could, and you know it. He's not such an angel as you make him out to be. He's *just* like me, Vega dearest. Don't forget, the same blood flows through our veins."

At that, something inside me coiled tightly, threatening to snap. *Callum would never murder people like you do!*

I wanted to scream.

Her eyes glistened as she smiled, anticipating the tirade gestating in my mind. I was so ready to unleash a stream of insults at her—curse words that I'd never flung at anyone in my entire life.

But instead, I swallowed, told myself to take a deep breath, and said, "You need to step down, Isla. You aren't the rightful queen—you never were. The violence must end today, for the good of the Otherwhere." With that, I glanced at Lumus, who was staring me down with his usual cold intensity. "You two can live a peaceful, quiet life somewhere—both of you."

"What in all the worlds," the queen purred, stepping toward me, "makes you think, *girl*, that I would ever want to live a quiet life?"

I glared at her, standing my ground as she moved closer and closer. "Are you seriously asking me that question?" I snarled, gesturing, arms out, to the space around us. "What do you call this life of isolation? You have no friends. You've destroyed the city that surrounds this castle. You've ruined your own domain, and your only allies are Waergs—who probably despise you deep down—and Ursals who *definitely* despise you. Wouldn't you two rather live your lives away from those who abhor you?"

"Every leader has haters," Isla said. "The more a leader is despised, the more powerful they prove themselves to be."

"Then you must be extremely powerful, *indeed*."

"Enough!"

It wasn't the queen who reacted now, but Lumus who shot a hand out, a bolt of lightning crackling its way through the air toward me.

I countered it, raising my palm against the spell, and the warlock's projectile froze in mid-air. I moved toward it, examining its quivering electricity as it struggled in vain to escape the clutches of my power.

With a wave of my hand, the projectile shattered like delicate glass and fell, useless, to the ground, its shards spreading like spilled water.

I suppressed a gasp of shock.

I'd become powerful over the months and accomplished things I had never imagined possible. But I...I didn't know I could do *that*.

Had Merriwether had a hand in my spell casting? Was he watching us through the Orb of Kilarin? Did he somehow know I was in trouble?

I raised my eyes to Lumus, who looked as stunned as I felt.

There was something else in his expression, too. I saw fear in him—terror of what I had become and what I had the potential to do to him, but also to his wife and his son.

"You're improving," he said, pushing away his expression and concealing it behind a veil of disdain. "Of course, on the open field, you will have many distractions. It won't be so easy for you when your people are being savaged by an army of beasts. And trust me—our Ursals will take your fellow Academy trainees with ease."

"What is your goal?" I asked, my chin held high even though my hands were now shaking. "Why do you two want so badly to destroy these lands?"

"Destroy?" Lumus asked, his voice thin and hostile at once. "You misunderstand. Isla and I wish to *rebuild* the Otherwhere.

We intend to create a new land, one with no Academy for the Blood-born and no Covens. All Witches will be forced to marry and bear children—as women are meant to do. All those who reside in our lands will have a choice: be banished to hide in the shadows or submit to the queen. Grells will work as servants to humans and Waergs alike. Wizards will take a vow never to rise up against us, or they will die. *That* is a peaceful world—one without war and conflict. It is a world in which the hierarchy is clearly laid out—one where no one will complain, because every citizen will know their place."

"Sounds to me like a world where you enslave and oppress those you don't like."

Lumus laughed. "Sometimes, these things are necessary to maintain the peace. A leader must make difficult decisions, you know—or had you not realized it already? Your grandfather, for instance."

"What about him?"

Lumus' malevolent grin intensified. "You worship him, don't you? You think he's the essence of goodness. But your grandfather has killed on more than a few occasions. You see, Vega—no one is purely good or evil. We all reside on a spectrum. It's really only a question of perspective."

I let out a laugh then, something uncontrolled and guttural, and Lumus flinched. Only for a second, but I saw it.

Mockery drives him mad. He's just like his son...

"You really think you can compare yourself to Merriwether," I said. It wasn't a question. Lumus and my grandfather were nothing alike, regardless of what the warlock might try to make me believe.

"No," Lumus said. "There is no comparison between us. I am far superior to him, both in mind and body—as you will discover soon enough."

"Do you really think, Vega dear," the queen interrupted before I could ask what he meant, "that the Otherwhere will become a lovely place of peace and tranquility if Callum takes the throne? Do you not see that it will still have the same troubles it has always had? Callum is soft. He's weak. Whether you like it or not, you know the truth: Under my reign, this land has been peaceful—that is, until you and yours decided to steal the Relics."

"The Relics are the domain of Seekers. They exist to keep order and balance in this land, and you know it."

"Order!" Isla cried out, her voice violent as it echoed around the chamber. "They exist out of pure vanity. They exist so that you high-and-mighty Blood-born can keep yourselves convinced of your importance. And that bloody awful grandfather of yours. If he would stop meddling in our affairs, perhaps we could end this war before too many more die. But he's intent on placing my brother on the throne, which would be disastrous. So can you blame me for trying to stop him? Tell me—what would you do in my place?"

From anyone else, I might have taken the question at face value. But from Isla, it seemed like a dig. A jab into my ribs with an invisible blade.

I glowered at her for a moment, my cheeks heating with rage.

"Is that a trick question?" I asked. "Do you think for a moment that I would agree that it's a bad idea to set Callum on the throne? I *know* his leadership skills. I know his power. He is exactly the sort of king this land needs."

Isla scoffed, "His power lies solely with his dragon. Trust me—once Caffall is dead, my brother will be little more than a useless mortal."

Panic seized at my chest.

Caffall, dead?

That's their plan?

"His dragon is part of him!" I yelled, my voice trembling with emotion. "You *can't* kill him. It would…"

The queen laughed. "It would kill my brother?" she asked, faux-sweetness ugly on her voice. "What a shame that would be."

I'd heard enough.

It was time to leave. To return to Callum, to throw my arms around him. To warn him and Caffall of his sister's intentions.

But first, I had one more thing to say.

"I want you to know that I will do everything in my power to take you both down," I told them, my eyes moving from one to the other. "If it means killing you both, I will do it. I may be a Seeker—but I am also a great deal more, and I will not let you hurt Callum or Caffall. If I have to die to see them rise to their rightful place, then so be it."

"We look forward to seeing you die, then," Lumus said, bowing low in mockery.

I sneered at him, then disappeared.

25
BACK TO THE ROSE WING

Hard gasps erupted from my chest as I found myself standing in our living room in the Rose Wing.

Within a matter of seconds Callum was in front of me, an expression of deep concern set in his eyes.

"Vega—what is it? What's happened?"

I shook my head, unwilling to speak at first. But I had to—I needed to tell him what they'd said about him, about Caffall.

If I'd harbored any illusions that war wasn't fully upon us before speaking to the queen and Lumus, they were long gone now.

She'd said herself that her army was heading this way. All our lives were hanging by a thread...and it was time to make some difficult decisions.

I took Callum by the hands, my eyes hot with tears that I cursed as they slipped down my cheeks.

"They want to kill Caffall!" I blurted out. "They want to weaken you, and they're convinced Caffall is the secret to your strength. *That's* your sister's plan."

"My sister?" he echoed. "Wait—you went to see Isla?"

I nodded, still fighting back tears of rage, of fear, and of sadness.

"I'm sorry," I said. "I know you would have told me not to—"

"Damned right I would have!" he snapped. "What the hell were you thinking, Vega?"

I pulled away, shocked by his tone. My brows met, my anger refocused, now aimed at him. "I was *thinking*," I said, my tone hard, "that I could negotiate with her. She sent a Waerg looking for me in Fairhaven, so I went to Uldrach. And for the record, I don't need your permission to make decisions. You're not the king yet, you know."

The last words were snarky, and I knew it. But I was in no mood for anyone, not even Callum, to talk to me like I was a fool.

"I'm sorry," he said, his tone softening. "You're right. And even if I should become king, you would never need to ask my permission. I was just…afraid for you, Vega. If Isla and Lumus want me weakened, they know the easiest way to injure my soul would be to hurt you. It was dangerous, what you did."

"I know," I said, remorseful. "But they didn't try to hurt me. At least, not really."

"What exactly does that mean?"

"Lumus cast a spell, and I stopped it," I confessed. "He looked a little surprised that I managed it."

Callum pulled back, his brow creasing more. But then, a strange thing happened.

He laughed.

"What's funny?" I asked.

"It's no wonder they're talking about taking Caffall down," he said, still chuckling. "They've realized Vega Sloane is untouchable, but the golden dragon, on the other hand…" He snickered.

"I'm serious, Callum. They want to kill him."

"I know," he replied. "I know. I've expected this for a long time. Isla would never find the strength of character to stab me in the chest, but she'll happily destroy the very thing that makes me...*me*. That means taking Caffall down, which would be like tearing out my heart. But she doesn't seem to understand that she'll have to go through me to get to him."

"We can't let it happen! We have to warn Caffall. We have to—"

But when Callum stared back at me with an amused look, I understood.

"He knows," I said, blowing out a long breath, my chest deflating. "You've already warned him."

He nodded. "Of course I have. But to tell you the truth, I don't think my sister really cares about Caffall. She just wants to instill enough fear in me that I'll agree to stop pursuing the throne. Isla is and has always been a fearful creature. She's terrified of me, but most of all, she's afraid of change. She has always wanted to rule the Otherwhere with a fist of steel—even if it means every man, woman, Grell, and child in this realm despises her. In her ideal world, I would leave this land never to look back. I would go to your world and live there, happily ever after, with you. Which, honestly, isn't such a terrible prospect. Sometimes, I daydream about living in your nice home in Fairhaven, lying on the couch with you while you stroke my hair and we watch movies about worlds that exist only in the human imagination."

"But you can't leave the Otherwhere!" I protested. "You...Caffall..."

"Don't worry, Vega—I know what would happen. I know it's impossible. But sometimes it's nice to dream of impossible things."

I stepped forward and wrapped my arms around him. I wanted to hold on for years and never let go.

I wanted to skip the war that was coming.

Fairhaven was my home, and in many ways, it would always be.

But Callum could never live there.

Which meant I could either stay with him in the Otherwhere or leave him and return to my world—and lose him.

I was beginning to think that no matter what happened, there would be no real happy ending. Not for me.

But I couldn't think about the end. Not yet. For now, I had to focus on the queen and on how to beat her.

I threw myself down on the couch, my head resting against the ridge at its back, and said, "Ugh. Why is she like this? Why does she love driving everyone mad with her threats? The damage she does, it's…"

"Unforgivable," Callum said. "*She's* unforgivable. I hate her for all of it—but mostly, I hate her for everything she's put you through."

"I could have killed her today," I said almost absently. "I wanted to."

When it sank in that I'd uttered those words, my eyes widened in shock. Had I really just said that? Had I just told Callum that I wanted to take his sister's life?

"I'm sorry," I stammered. "I don't know why I said that."

"I do. It's because that's what my sister deserves for everything she's done." Callum plopped down next to me, and for a moment I felt like I had when he and I first knew each other—when we were nothing more than a couple of teenagers. It was a simpler time. A wonderful, peaceful, happy time.

Even if was all an illusion.

Those were days when we felt like two people falling in love, getting to know one another without the weight of the world on our shoulders. It saddened me to think we might never have days like those again, regardless of the outcome of this war.

The best-case scenario meant Callum would become king—which meant carefree days would be few and far between.

And I didn't even want to *think* about the worst-case scenario.

"What are we going to do?" I asked, leaning my head against

his shoulder. "How do we fix this broken thing that is the Otherwhere?"

"We have to win," he said, his voice low. He spoke the words as if winning was the simplest thing in the world. "We have no choice. If we lose this war, I can't even imagine what will happen to the Otherwhere."

"*I* can imagine," I said with a shudder. "We've both seen the Chasm and the lands beyond. We know what destructive powers like Lumus's can do to this realm."

Callum kissed the top of my head, then nodded. "Yes. But I have no intention of letting that happen. I intend to restore the south—to heal the lands beyond the Chasm. I want the Otherwhere to return to the beautiful place it once was. In the meantime, I'll do what I can to keep my sister from taking one more life. I will fight until I'm dead if that's what it takes."

I pulled back to look at him, my eyes stinging with tears. "Stop," I said. "Don't say things like that. Not ever. You're everything—not just to me, but to this land, whether the people know it or not. You can't die. You and Caffall need to live—to thrive."

Callum offered up a frown. "Don't worry. I have no intention of dying. But we do need a plan. Something more than just brawn. We have our Zerkers, our Healers, our Rangers. We have you and Merriwether. But I'm afraid we still need more."

"We have the Grells, the dragons, and the Witches," I said. "And we have the Relics."

As I spoke those words, a sound met my ears.

No, not my ears.

The sound reverberated somewhere deep in my mind, like the distant, imagined shattering of glass.

"Did you hear that?" I asked, leaping to my feet.

Callum was next to me in an instant, shaking his head, but I could tell he was intent on knowing what I was talking about.

"What is it?" he asked. "Tell me."

"Something has broken," I said, looking up into his light eyes.

"Something that wasn't meant to break. It probably sounds insane, but..."

"But what?" he said gently. "Tell me."

"I *felt* it. It was here, in the Academy—but far from the Rose Wing." I took his hand. "I have to find Merriwether. Will you come with me?"

"I'm not letting you out of my sight after everything that's happened."

"Good."

In an instant, we were in my grandfather's office. He was seated in his desk chair, a look of quiet worry in his eyes.

"Ah, you two," he said when he saw us, rising to his feet. "I wish I could say I was surprised to see you. I'm sorry to tell you, but it's happened."

"What's happened? What was that sound?" I asked, my voice strained with concern.

"The Lightsmith has broken free of his prison," he said. "He's left the Academy. But before he left...it seems that he did a little damage."

26
DESTRUCTION

I practically jogged to keep up with Callum and Merriwether as they strode toward the staircase that would lead us down to the Academy's dungeon.

"What do you mean, the Lightsmith broke free?" I asked breathlessly. "How could he have escaped? I thought—"

"You thought I was strong enough to hold him within the Academy's walls," Merriwether said, his voice irritatingly calm. "You thought he would never again walk under the sun."

"Of course I did!" I cried as we stormed past a series of Zerkers in their red uniforms, eyeing us curiously as we moved. "I thought that was the point—to keep him here, at least until the war was won."

I didn't want to say what I was really thinking. Had the Lightsmith bested my grandfather? Was he stronger than Merriwether?

If he was, did any of us really stand a chance?

"That was never the point, my dear granddaughter," Merriwether said, turning briefly to offer up a look I couldn't entirely read.

But I could see that he was enjoying this—whatever this was—far too much. And it was clear he wasn't about to give me any straight answers.

I took Callum's arm and whispered, "Do you have any idea what he's talking about?"

"No," he admitted. "Then again, I rarely do. But your grandfather always seems to know what he's doing, so I'm choosing to suppress my curiosity."

As much as I admired his ability to bite his tongue, I was utterly lacking in that area. Any filter I'd once possessed had abandoned me, and I was too aggravated to put on a façade of calm.

"The Lightsmith is dangerous!" I practically shouted. "He killed a Witch!"

"He did," Merriwether agreed. "And I haven't forgotten it."

There was a finality in his voice as he uttered those words—something dark and ire-filled, and he said nothing more.

We advanced in silence until we arrived at the end of a long corridor of stone. I glanced around to realize I'd never been in this part of the Academy—never seen this particular corner before. It looked like a dead end—a wall of gray, cold rock standing in our way. But when the Headmaster waved his hand and spoke a few words under his breath, the stone faded to nothing and we stepped forward, a sense of damp cold engulfing us.

"Vega," Merriwether said, stopping and turning to face me, "one day, perhaps you will need to find your way here—but let us hope it won't be for many years. In the meantime, memorize this place. Know it. You will be the only one who can access it after I'm gone."

There was so much meaning in those words—so much I didn't want to confront. Merriwether, gone from the Academy? No. I couldn't imagine it.

Was he talking about his death?

Surely not.

Merriwether was ageless—at least, in his own unique "how old can he possibly be?" way. I couldn't even imagine him dying.

Not soon.

Not ever.

Stop overthinking everything, I told myself. *Snap out of it, Vega.*

I nodded in silence, and we continued along our way as Merriwether lifted a hand, illuminating the space before us with a series of torches along each wall.

Finally, we arrived at a door—at least, the remnants of a door. It was made of solid, thick wood and iron, and now hung off its hinges as though a massive fist had cleft it in two.

"This was his cell?" I asked, my legs trembling beneath me. I didn't want to see the Lightsmith again. And even the thought of entering his cell was more horrifying than I'd imagined.

"No," Merriwether said. "This was the entrance to the Academy's vault—at least, *one* of them. This was where I stored three of the four Relics of Power. The Orb, as you know, is hidden elsewhere."

I was beginning to wonder how wise it had been to keep the Relics together, so easily accessible by the enemy.

For that matter, how wise had it been to bring the Lightsmith here at all?

But when we stepped through the broken door into the next room—a small chamber of stone—and saw what the Lightsmith had done, my questions faded quickly.

All I felt now was confusion...and fear.

Set into the far wall was another door, this one made entirely of thick, seemingly unbreakable iron. Yet it was shattered into pieces, some of which were now scattered on the floor inside the vault.

When Merriwether stepped forward, I froze, fear consuming

me. Callum seemed to sense it and put an arm around me, pulling me silently close.

"I'm so sorry I wasn't there," he said. "When you saw him on the road—when he…"

I nodded, sorrow for the Witch I had never met sending a pulse of pain through my chest.

"He's gone," Callum whispered. "The Lightsmith isn't here. Merriwether would never put you in harm's way—you have nothing to fear."

"I know," I said. "It's just—I should have stopped him, and I was too scared. I should have attacked him. I could have summoned creatures to do it for me. But I didn't. I just…froze."

"Anyone would have done the same, given the circumstances."

"The Witches didn't. The reason Clio died was because she had the courage to confront him."

"That's only because she didn't truly know what he was capable of, Vega. You felt how dangerous he was. You understood him as Clio couldn't."

"Callum is right," Merriwether said, eyeing the damage. "But there's something more to it, as well."

"What's that?" I asked, my voice trembling.

Merriwether turned to me, kindness in his eyes. "You didn't only freeze out of fear, Vega. You may not realize it—you may not have known it then. But you froze because some part of you knew the Lightsmith needed to live."

"I don't understand."

"Come, Granddaughter. Look."

I stepped cautiously toward Merriwether, Callum by my side, until I understood what it was that had sounded like shattering glass inside my mind.

"Oh, my God," I breathed.

On the ground, scattered into tiny fragments, was the Scepter of Morgana—one of the four Relics. The very item we'd used to save Callum and Caffall after they'd been split apart.

"How did I hear this shattering all the way from the Rose Wing?"

"Because you are connected to the Relics," Merriwether said, laying a hand on my shoulder. "You're a Seeker—the strongest of them. You *felt* the Scepter's demise."

"Demise? You mean it's really gone? It won't reappear in fifty years, as it always has?"

"It's been broken down by the smith," Merriwether confirmed. "When the Lightsmith destroys, it's for good. He can create, too, if he so chooses—but he will not bring back the scepter. Its time in this world has ended."

I glanced around to see that the sword, too—the legendary sword that once belonged to Arthur Pendragon and was known as Excalibur—was broken. But instead of shattering it into many shards, the Lightsmith had simply snapped its blade in two.

The Lyre of Adair, on the other hand, was wholly intact, sitting on a stone table at the far end of the small chamber.

"None of this makes sense," I said. "Why would he break two of the Relics, but not the third? And why did he only break the sword's blade in two? And where did he go?"

"If you want to know the answer to the final question, summon the Orb of Kilarin," Merriwether replied.

Without hesitation I did as he said, calling to the Orb to come to me. It appeared a moment later, hovering in the air above my open palms.

"Tell me where the Lightsmith is," I said. "Is he going to the queen?"

A cloud of smoke consumed the Orb for a moment, then cleared to reveal a figure on the open road, moving swiftly across country. But he wasn't headed to the castle Uldrach.

Instead, he was headed north, toward the mountains.

"It is my belief," Merriwether said with a strange sigh, "that he's trying to tell us something." He looked oddly unconcerned, like he'd been expecting this. "This act of destruction—and preservation—was deliberate."

"You..." I said, hesitating for a moment before speaking again, a revelation unfolding in my mind. "You brought him to the Academy because you knew this would happen. You knew he would destroy at least one Relic—didn't you?"

Callum looked back and forth between us, baffled.

"What?" he said. "Merriwether, why would you allow this to happen, after everything the Seekers went through?"

"Because he wanted the Lightsmith to tell us how to win the war," I said slowly, the answer coming to me like a figure striding out of thick mist to reveal itself.

Merriwether grinned, though there was pain in his eyes. "Correct," he said. "At least, I'd *hoped* for an answer. As I've said, the Lightsmith is a creature of instinct. He is neither human nor beast. But he has dwelled for many years in these lands. The Otherwhere is his home. It always has been, and always will be. Destroying all of the Relics would have meant our downfall, and he knew it. And if the Academy falls, so does the Otherwhere—which means his home would be destroyed too, wherever it may lie. He knows the queen will leave no one standing when her forces rampage across the land—not unless we manage to stop them."

"Surely you're not trying to tell us he's good," Callum said angrily. "You're not trying to claim he's our ally, after all he's done!"

"He's no one's ally," Merriwether snapped, a warning in his voice. "Not ours, not your sister's. He doesn't think in those terms. He only wants to live, to breathe, like so many of us. And he has offered us a gift today."

"How?" Callum spat. "How is it a gift to destroy the Scepter and the sword?"

"The sword is not destroyed," Merriwether said, picking up the pieces of the weapon that was so famous, even in my world.

"It can and will be reforged—and will be made stronger than it ever was before. The Lightsmith knew this when he broke its blade. He *wanted* it reforged."

"And the Lyre of Adair?" I asked. "Why leave it intact?"

"Because the Lyre can call forth an army, if it finds its way to the right hands." Merriwether spoke those words with a twinkle in his eye, as if he knew precisely whose hands he was talking about. "The time will come soon enough for its player to appear. But for now," he said, reaching down to take the sword's hilt and broken blade in hand, "I must bring this to the smithy. The queen's army is close, and it's almost time to do battle."

"How close?" I asked, my fear renewed as I recalled what the Usurper Queen had said.

"Look to the Orb. Ask it."

I did as he said, and when the image came to me, my breath caught in my chest.

The army of Ursals and Waergs had reached the foothills, less than a day's ride from where we now stood.

We would soon be caught up in a full-on war.

"We have to warn everyone!" I said. "The dragons are still far away, and the Grells…"

"The Grells have been awaiting my signal. As for the dragons, are you forgetting you're a Summoner, my dear?"

The truth was, I *had* almost forgotten. I could call the dragons to my side with a mere few words.

"What do we do?" I asked. "How do we…"

"Fight?"

I nodded.

"The Academy is well fortified, but we still can't risk an all-out attack on these walls, or this institution will fall. We must bring the fight to the enemy. So, at dawn tomorrow, that's precisely what we'll do." Merriwether shot a look toward Callum. "You must ensure Caffall is with you and ready."

"And the sword?"

"It will end up precisely where it needs to be—in the hands of the one meant to wield it."

Callum nodded understanding.

"Vega," Merriwether added, "we will send word to the Witches and your friend Lachlan. It's vital that they be here when the battle begins."

I nodded. "Of course. But…why Lachlan?"

He was Callum's cousin, after all, and in line to the throne. I couldn't help but think maybe it would be wisest to keep him away—to give him a chance at survival, in case the worst should happen.

"You'll see soon enough," Merriwether said.

I gawked at him for a few seconds, then said, "You've seen the outcome of the war in the Orb, haven't you? That's why you're being so shifty about this."

"I've seen a thousand possible outcomes," he replied. "Most are unlikely. What I know with certainty is that we need to manufacture our own luck. And the only way to do so is to ensure the right pieces are in place before we make our final move."

"*Final?*" Callum said. "We haven't even made our first move yet."

"Oh, Mr. Drake," Merriwether chuckled. "We've been making moves for years now, and you know it. When you first encountered Vega in the bookshop in Fairhaven, that was a move. When she first encountered your sister—when she shared the title of Chosen Seeker with the others? All were brilliant moves in this game. We are now at the end. And if all goes well, we will soon be declared winners. But for that, we will need help. We aren't alone, regardless of how isolated we may feel just now."

"I still don't know what we're meant to do," I lamented. "Aside from fight tooth and nail."

"Then fight tooth and nail we will. But our battlefield will not only be the plains of the Otherwhere, I'm afraid. There is a final battle coming—one that will be far more gruesome." Merriwether sighed as if exhaustion had just overtaken him. "Now, come. You two need to rest. Tomorrow will be the most difficult day of your lives."

"But no pressure," I said. "Right?"

27
CALM BEFORE THE STORM

In the Rose Wing's living room, I paced back and forth, biting my nails.

It was a habit my mother had once had. Whenever she was apprehensive—which wasn't often—she drove my father to distraction by chewing on her nails until he quietly begged her to stop.

"It helps me think," she insisted.

Those words were enough to satisfy him.

And now, Callum didn't even need to ask why I was chewing frantically. He knew as well as anyone what was on my mind.

"The Sword of Viviane," I said after I'd crossed the living room floor for the hundredth time. "The Lyre of Adair. They're important. Why won't Merriwether explain why?"

Callum, who had been sitting watching me from the couch, rose to his feet and stepped over to me, blocking my way. I stopped, my eyes locking onto his. For a moment, I was transported back to the first time we'd met in the Novel Hovel in Fairhaven. The instant when I had fallen for him on the most superficial of levels—before falling for him on the deepest one.

"Magic always finds a way," he said softly, slipping his fingers under my chin. "Whether we like surrendering to it or not, we're at the mercy of it now. Since Uther Pendragon, since the days of King Arthur and Morgan Le Fay, magic has ruled this land. We *have* to put our trust in Merriwether. We must believe in the sword and the Lyre—and the Orb. But most of all, we need to trust our instincts."

At that, a cry arose that pierced through the Academy's thick stone walls, and for a split-second, my blood froze. My mind spun with horrid thoughts. Were the queen's forces moving faster than I'd feared? Would they attack tonight?

But after a few seconds, I registered the familiarity of the cry and darted to the balcony alongside Callum to see Caffall soaring in circles outside, his eyes fixed on the lands beyond the Academy's walls.

When he saw us, he banked hard and flew toward us, halting some distance from the balcony to flap his wings slowly, his eyes locked on us both.

"What have you seen?" I asked the golden dragon.

I'd almost forgotten how beautiful he was, how intelligent his eyes, how exquisite his gleaming scales. To think the queen wanted to hurt such a creature broke my heart.

~A host of Waergs and Ursals are making their way along the main road, Caffall said, his deep voice speaking directly to my mind and to Callum's. *And some humans, as well. They seem to have stopped for the night and have set up camp a few hours away, but I have little doubt they'll be on the move soon.*

"We need to call to the other dragons," I said, turning to Callum, who nodded. "Dachmal, Tefyr, and the others. I can bring them here."

"I'm afraid you're right," Callum said. "Caffall—do you know where they are?"

The dragon, expressionless as his face was, looked lost for a moment. *~I'm afraid not,* he replied. *They were fighting in the North, but when I flew up to call them to my side, they had disappeared. The*

Waergs they had fought had been slaughtered, the Ursals dead or run off. I suppose the dragons left when they were no longer needed.

"They won their battle, then," I said with a sigh of relief. "Still, I need to find them—to make sure they're all right."

I backed into the living room and summoned the Orb of Kilarin, which twisted in the air before me.

"Show me Dachmal," I commanded, and the Orb did as I asked, smoke at its center clearing to reveal the blue dragon.

"He's…flying," I said. "Somewhere dark. Not surprising, I suppose. It's night all over the Otherwhere. Still…"

I asked the Orb to back away a little so that I could see if the other four dragons were with Dachmal. I could only see Tefyr, his silver companion. It seemed they'd separated from the others.

As my eyes moved back to Dachmal, a strange shape pulled my gaze to his silhouette.

"Someone is on his back," I said, my voice tight.

Dachmal was powerful, as were all dragons. He didn't let just anyone on his back. In fact, I'd always thought no one outside of our alliance would ever be allowed to ride him.

Something about the outline of the figure on his back unsettled me, though I couldn't be certain who it was.

Dismissing the Orb, I tried calling to Dachmal with my mind and summoning him to the large courtyard below our balcony.

But when I reached out to him, all I received in return was grim silence.

"Something is wrong," I said, turning to Callum. "He's never ignored my call. Never. Whoever was riding him…what if it was Lumus?"

For a millisecond, I saw a look of horror cross Callum's normally stoic face. But he pushed it aside, shook his head, and said, "We shouldn't speculate. Dachmal is strong, as are the other dragons. Let's hope whoever he's with, he's all right. Chances are you can't communicate with him because he's occupied with another ally.

~*I can hunt for them, if you like,* Caffall offered.

"No," Callum replied. "You need to rest—and stay close. We will head out at dawn to confront the queen's forces."

For a moment, Caffall seemed to lower his head in a gesture of sadness—or remorse. I could only imagine the pain he would feel if an enemy really had taken control of Dachmal, and he had to fight his fellow dragons.

But I couldn't console him—couldn't tell him it wouldn't be necessary. The truth was, I had no idea how we would survive the coming dawn and all it brought.

All I knew was that I had to hold onto the few shreds of hope in my chest.

~*I will rest, then,* Caffall said. *I'll await your summons in the morning.* His eyes seemed to move to mine when he added, ~*Do not despair, Vega Sloane. Prophecies always find a way. The heir will find his throne, and all will be well.*

"How many have to die before that happens?" I asked, my voice twisting inside my chest.

~*If the right enemies are dealt with,* the dragon said, *then their underlings will scatter. Vanquish the leader, and the war will be easily won.*

With that, he banked and flew down to the courtyard, tucking himself into a dark corner for the night like a roosting pigeon.

I stared down at him, then at the shadows of the courtyard, at the sky above us, the distant hills of the Otherwhere...and I trembled.

Sensing my fear, Callum came up behind me, wrapped his arms around me, and whispered, "Gold coin for your thoughts."

"If I told you what I was thinking, it would make the fear too real."

"Then tell me something else," he said, pressing his chin to the waves of hair atop my head. "Tell me something you're looking forward to."

Looking forward. If only I felt confident that I would live past the next twenty-four hours, so that it even made sense to look forward.

I wanted to weep at the thought that I hadn't said a proper goodbye to those I'd left behind in my world.

"I'm looking forward to visiting my brother and my Nana," I said. "I'm looking forward to seeing Will's face again, hearing his voice—to feeling normal and not in fear that so many people and creatures that I love will die."

I turned around to face Callum, who looked down at me with all the love in this world or any other behind his eyes. He reached down and touched his fingertip to my ring, its red stones glowing in the faint light.

"I'm going to make you a promise right now," he said. "And you might think I don't mean it, but I do."

I hesitated, then said, "Tell me."

"I promise you, Vega Sloane, that you will see your brother and your Nana at my coronation. I promise to do everything in my power to ensure the safety of as many Zerkers, Healers, Rangers, and others on our side as possible. And after it's all over, I promise to give you the most beautiful life you can imagine."

I watched as his finger slid over my ring, which sparked to life under his touch as if sensing a power in him that was intangible and unquestionable.

"*If* you still want me when all this is done," he added.

Callum had always been careful not to pressure me. He had so often tried to protect me from my own fate—to keep me from having to choose between my love for him and my love for my old life.

Right now, the frightened girl in me wanted to run back to my world, where my fellow Seekers were probably tucked comfortably into their beds, sleeping soundly. Their work in the Otherwhere was done now—and under any other circumstances, mine would have been, too.

But I had a grandfather in this land. I had a duty.

And I had Callum.

I loved him. I had loved him since the first moment we'd met. And now, having been through so much together and apart, I couldn't imagine my life without him.

Whatever I had to do to survive, I would do it. And after that, whatever I needed to do to keep him in my life...I would do that, too.

"I want you now," I said. "I will *always* want you, Callum. I can't imagine a world or a time when I wouldn't." I pulled my hand up and cupped his cheek, the ring flashing still brighter as I touched him. "I promise you—at the end of all this, if we're both still standing, I will be by your side at your coronation."

"And then?" he asked. "Do you see yourself remaining in the Otherwhere?"

At that, I pulled back.

It was such a complicated question. If I remained, I wouldn't age as I would in my own world. Time was different here, and eventually, after years spent with Callum, I could return to Fairhaven looking as I always had—a young woman of eighteen, while everyone else had aged naturally.

How would I ever explain something like that? What if Will married and had children? How would he explain that his sister never aged without telling them the truth?

"We'll cross that bridge when we come to it," I said, more to myself than to him.

"I see," he said, pulling away. In his eyes I could see the pain of rejection, so I grabbed his arm and said, "That's not what I meant. I was thinking of how I could tell the people at home about all of it. Because Callum—you *are* my future...if I'm lucky enough to have one. You and this land. This is where I want to be." I let out a little laugh, and it felt good. "How could I possibly ever walk away from you? No one would ever come close to making me feel like you do."

His pain seemed to diminish, but something in him was still

reserved. "You could meet someone down the road, Vega," he said.

"Yes, I could," I agreed. "But he wouldn't be part-dragon, would he?"

At that, Callum finally laughed. "Does this mean what I think it does?" he asked, eyeing the ring once again. "Are you saying…"

"I'm saying that after we win this nonsense war against your sister—after you're crowned—and after you beg for Will's blessing…"

"Yes?"

"I'll consider being your official girlfriend."

"Tease!" he said, taking me by the waist, pulling me close, and kissing me.

It was so good to feel normal, if only for a moment. To feel like we could laugh and joke around—like the world wasn't about to end.

And as Callum kissed me for the thousandth time, I felt that sensation I always craved when I was in his presence. The floor melted below me, and I sank down deep, deep into some place where no one—not even my greatest enemies—could touch me.

28

DAWN

I AWOKE TO THE SOUND OF HORNS BLARING IN THE DISTANCE, THEIR cry as fierce as the howl of a Waerg.

Callum was already awake and dressed, standing at attention at the window. Caffall was circling in the sky beyond, enormous wings flapping in the dim light of the breaking dawn.

"He tells me he can see the enemy's forces several miles from here," Callum said. "I hate to say it...but it's time."

Nausea swelled inside me as reality hit.

I was so afraid. Not as much for myself as for everyone else in the Otherwhere. For the women, men, and children who had lost their lives to the encroaching army. For those who would soon die.

For those who would suffer the loss of loved ones.

I refused to admit that I could be one of the victims of this war.

I have a role to play, I told myself. *And it's not death. Not today.*

I dressed quickly, rushing over to the window.

"I need to summon Solara," I said. "To tell her to call the Witches to our aid."

"No need," Callum said, nodding, his eyes locked on the courtyard.

I looked down to see Solara standing with Lachlan, Lily and Merriwether, as well as several other Witches from the Aradia Coven. At Solara's waist was a long-sheathed sword, its hilt intertwined silver and gold. The weapon was exquisite and made her look even more daunting than usual.

"The Sword of Viviane?" I asked softly, squinting. "Merriwether said it would be reforged. But that doesn't look like its hilt."

"It's not," Callum replied, pointing outside. "Where the sword is, I can't say. But I suspect our beloved Headmaster knows."

"Eat something before we head out," Callum said, turning to me and slipping a finger under my chin. "Then go down to the courtyard to join the others. I'm going to ride out on Caffall, and we'll do what we can to stop the enemy from advancing any further." He kissed me gently, then said, "I love you, you know."

"I know," I replied, swallowing down the emotions surging inside my chest and throat. "I love you, too."

I wanted to say what was really on my mind—the words that would make a coward of me. "Don't go, please. Stay here with me, where it's safe."

But I knew perfectly well the Academy wouldn't be safe much longer—not unless Callum, Caffall, and our small army all made our way out there.

If ever there had been a time for Callum to show his leadership skills, this was it.

When he'd kissed me one last time then headed out the Rose Wing's main door to go find Caffall, I forced down a little bread, fruit, and water. Swallowing hard, I transported myself outside, where I found Merriwether and the others.

"What's the plan?" I asked, clasping my hands nervously together.

"We head out to confront them head-on," Merriwether said.

"The Orb has told me the enemies' numbers are great, so we can only hope our allies arrive in time. The Rangers from the northern lands are close, as are several Zerker and Caster forces from the scattered cities. But perhaps now is the time to summon our friends, the dragons."

My heart sank at those words, and I stared up at my grandfather, realizing I hadn't yet told him what had happened.

"I tried to call Dachmal last night," I said, my voice apologetic. "Callum and I...we saw him in the Orb, with someone on his back." I glanced at Solara, wincing as I spoke. "He didn't respond when I called to him."

Merriwether's brows met, more out of concern than anger. "Vega—why didn't you tell me this?"

"I...I suppose I forgot," I stammered, daunted by his expression. "I can call him again. I might have been mistaken—it's possible all I saw was a shadow. He was probably just fighting in the North with the others."

Merriwether took me by the shoulders, his fingers gripping me hard—though not so hard as to hurt. "Tell me...what happened when you called to him?"

"Nothing," I said, shaking my head. But then I paused, closed my eyes, and added, "Fog. Thick and dark, like a veil over my mind. It was like he and I had been blocked from communicating with one another."

I opened my eyes to see that his worry had increased. "We will certainly need more than our usual allies, then," he said, looking at Solara, who nodded her understanding.

"Why? What's happened?" I cried. "Dachmal isn't in danger, is he?"

"The dragons have been corrupted," Merriwether said. "Someone has locked them into a spell. For now, they're beyond our reach. You and I can both guess who is behind this."

He was right about that.

The queen had stolen the dragons and caged them for a time,

and I had no doubt she would delight in taking hold of them once again for her own ends.

"Can't we do something to bring them back?" I asked. "Can't we break the spell?"

My grandfather shook his head. "We could—but only if we knew *exactly* where they were, and who was on Dachmal's back." He turned to look toward the Academy's gate. "There is someone we will summon in their stead, if the need should arise. One with the might of many dragons on his side. Hope is not lost."

"Who?" I asked, but already, Merriwether was marching toward the gates, raising his hands in the air.

A large, swirling portal formed before him, broader than the gates themselves, and taller. Within its depths I saw green, rolling hills, and I recognized them immediately.

The hills lay only a few miles west of the Academy.

It was there that the battle for our lives would begin.

29
READYING FOR WAR

"Soldiers of the Academy for the Blood-Born!" a booming, deep voice called out.

It took me a moment to realize it was Callum who spoke, commanding the troops from Caffall's back.

"Today, you will meet danger and glory—and some of you will meet death. But know that your sacrifices are in the name of the Otherwhere and all its people hold dear! You will not soon be forgotten. Your tales will be told in the tomes in the libraries across the Otherwhere and beyond. Now, we march to battle!"

I had never heard Callum speak in such a way. I'd seen him teach and lead, but not like this—not in the manner of a general at the head of a massive army.

I looked up at him, prouder than I'd ever been of the respect and admiration the soldiers had for him.

The Academy's amassed troops, too, watched him with tentative smiles on their faces, their chins held high. There were three hundred of them—not nearly as many as we needed.

But I reminded myself that we had others, too. Witches. Allies set to arrive from all over the realm.

Most reassuring of all, we had Callum, Caffall, and Merriwether.

I glanced at Solara, who had a look of determination set deep in her eyes.

"He's a good man," she said. "A great man. He will lead us to victory."

Her confidence fueled me, and I nodded, trying to absorb the sensation.

"Will you come with us, Vega?" she asked, nodding toward Lachlan, Lily, and the others, who were gathered at the courtyard's opposite end. "We'll need to fly. The ground troops can make their way through the portal, but I'd rather be airborne."

"Of course," I said, pulling my eyes to the sky and Caffall, who was now circling above us with Callum on his back. As I watched, the golden dragon banked and circled around again, his eyes locked on the distant point where I knew he could see an endless mass of the queen's fighting creatures.

How many are there? I asked silently.

~Four thousand, at least, Caffall's voice replied, his tone stoic. The dragon had never been a fearful creature. He spoke the number as if it was a mere inconvenience and not a death sentence.

I wished I knew that Dachmal and his friends were all right—that I could be sure that it wasn't the queen or Lumus I'd seen on Dachmal's back.

Somewhere above, a piercing sound cut through the air. I spun around, my feet planted firmly in the courtyard's soil, ready to cast a defensive spell against any encroaching forces. But after a second, I realized the terrifying sound had come from Caffall.

It was then that a sea of red-clad Zerkers began to storm through the portal in droves, followed by Rangers and Casters.

A familiar creature sprang toward us from among their ranks. It came to stop at my feet, rubbing his ferret-face against them.

"Rourke!" I said affectionately, happy beyond measure to know Niala must be close by.

Sure enough, she emerged from the crowd to head toward us.

"Are you ready?" she asked, giving me a quick hug.

"Is anyone ever ready for war?"

"Good point." Pulling back, she glanced skyward to Callum and Caffall. "I expected to see the other dragons. Where are they?"

My heart sank as I told her what I'd seen in the Orb.

"You have no idea who was riding Dachmal?"

"None. Only that I have a bad feeling about it. Dachmal is strong and unlikely to want anyone on his back, aside from a few select people—and all of those people are right here." I looked over her shoulder at a sea of Rangers moving toward the gates. "Aithan?" I asked, referring to the Ranger I'd met in the North—a Hawk shifter, and someone Niala cared deeply about. "Is he here?"

"He's with the Northerners, heading toward us," she replied, her cheeks flushing. "He sent a message to me last night via a razorbeak."

"A message?" I asked with a raised brow, forgetting for a moment where we were and what was about to happen. "Anything I should know about?"

"Let's just say that when my training at the Coven is finished, I intend to move to the North," she replied with a grin. "He likes it there, and I suspect I would, too."

My heart swelled to hear the hope in her voice, the unadulterated certainty that she would survive today's battle.

I needed to grant myself the gift of that same certainty.

There's no room for doubt, I told myself. *It won't help anyone.*

I squeezed Niala's hand then marched over to Merriwether, whose eyes were narrowed, locked on the forces he had helped train over the last several years as they passed through the portal.

"I feel ridiculous asking this now," I told him, "but what's the plan?"

"Our forces will march out to meet the enemy," he said without hesitation. "They'll confront the Ursals and the Waergs head-on—with the help of Callum, Caffall, and the rest of us."

"The enemy's army is so much bigger than ours, though," I said. "Do you really think we can—?"

At that he pulled his eyes to mine. For an instant, they brightened, giving his face the illusion of youth and vibrancy. "Of course I think we can win, Vega," he said with a smile. "If I didn't, I would send all the troops to the library, and there, we would have a final tea party together. But you see, we will win, because we must. We have no choice...which makes it quite simple, really."

Again, hope surged through me, and I allowed it to come. I welcomed it in.

All of a sudden, the air didn't smell so foul, the world didn't seem so grim.

"Come with me," Merriwether said, leaning down and whispering. "There's something I need to give you."

"Now?" I almost choked out. "The battle is about to start!"

"The battle can wait," Merriwether said with a calm that no one should have been capable of in that moment. "This will only take a moment."

He began to stride away from the others—away from our army that continued to pour through the portal.

I accompanied my grandfather as he moved silently toward a shadowy door on the courtyard's far side. I didn't ask where we were going, or why; I could already see that we were heading toward the Academy's smithy where the weapons, shields, and armor were forged.

"I'm hoping not to get close enough to the action to need armor," I insisted, and my grandfather chuckled. "Don't forget—I'm terrible with weapons."

"I'm well aware," he said with a wink. "But I still want you to have a weapon on hand—just in case."

I knew better than to question Merriwether's motives, so I forced my mouth shut until he had guided me over to a nearby anvil. Next to it stood a thick, round pillar of stone, and leaning against the pillar was a familiar object.

"The Sword of Viviane!" I said, leaping toward it.

Its blade was intact and gleaming bright silver, its hilt exquisitely polished. Next to it was a long sheath of black leather attached to an elegant, braided belt.

"Put it on, Vega," Merriwether said, taking hold of the weapon and sheathing it before handing it to me. "Keep it safe at all costs. It's here for a very important reason—it has a role to play today, and you are its keeper."

"But Callum should have it," I said. "He's King Arthur's descendant. It's only right."

"Ah, but he's high in the air on dragon-back, isn't he? A sword won't do him much good just now."

"I can call to Caffall," I insisted. "I can ask him to land…"

Merriwether shook his head. "Let Callum focus on riding the golden dragon. You need the blade by your side. Trust me on this one…Daughter of Viviane."

I winced at the last words, aware of what he was trying to tell me.

King Arthur had once wielded the sword, it was true. But my own ancestor had kept it safe long before then.

Viviane—*the Lady of the Lake,* as she was called.

It seemed I really was meant to be the weapon's keeper.

I strapped the belt around my waist—around the dark red tunic I had put on that morning over a pair of black leather trousers. I realized, smiling as I looked down at my attire, how similar it was to so much of what Solara wore.

"We'll make a Witch of you yet," Merriwether said, stepping back to take a look at me.

"If I were a Witch, I'd have to be part of a Coven," I replied, "and I wouldn't be able to…"

I stopped there, realizing what I was about to say.

"To marry Callum," Merriwether concluded. "It's true. Just as I never got to marry your grandmother. I don't recommend a lonely life. So perhaps you could be an *honorary* Witch instead."

I nodded silently.

I wondered sometimes how often he thought of Nana—how often they thought of one another, living as they did in two separate worlds.

But I already knew the answer:

Not a day—probably not even an hour—went by when they didn't think about one another.

"Chin up," Merriwether said, a hand on my shoulder to steer me toward the door and back to hard reality. "The world isn't as grim as you fear, you know. I still have high hopes for today."

"Why do I get the impression that you're about to implement a plan I'm not going to like?" I asked, mustering the weakest laugh.

"Because you know me well, Granddaughter. Now, let's get out there. It's time we dealt with some large bears."

30
BATTLEFIELD

I FLEW TO THE BATTLEFIELD ASTRIDE LACHLAN'S DRAKE AFTER promising I wouldn't disappear on him again.

At least, not without a warning.

~*Good*, he told me. *I'm going to hold you to that, you know, Vega.*

On any other day, I would probably have cracked a joke and asked him how, exactly, he intended to hold me to anything. Burn me with his drake-breath? Punch me with an adorable drake-fist? Threaten to redecorate my living room with tasteless furnishings?

Today, however, I was too busy freaking out to use humor as a coping mechanism. Maybe if we survived until morning, my smart-ass side would return.

Maybe.

In the distance, Caffall's enormous wings beat at the sky. Seeking to soothe my frayed nerves, I focused my eyes on Callum, at his gaze, trained as it was on the queen's distant forces.

When the enemy army came into view and the gruesome reality of the coming horror assaulted me fully, my heart sank like a boulder crashing into the deepest reaches of the sea.

Isla's forces spread over the landscape, a massive shadow infecting the Otherwhere's pastoral green lands. A scourge spreading far and wide, pulsing with malice.

From this distance, I could just barely make out the distinct outlines of the Ursals—hulking, threatening shapes that dwarfed the much smaller Waergs behind and beside them.

Rows of men and women marched behind the four-legged creatures, and I knew without asking that, though many of them were likely shifters, there were probably others among their numbers, too. Warlocks, Wizards, even the occasional rebel Witch or other Caster. The queen and Lumus had a way of drawing angry creatures of all sorts to their side, after all.

It didn't matter how many times I tried to convince myself we weren't walking into one of the more awful moments in the Otherwhere's history, a conflict that would change the lives of everyone present.

But I knew full well that whatever happened today would decide the fate of this land. Every small battle that had already occurred, every home burned, every life taken, had only been a prelude to the battle to come.

It seemed Lachlan could sense my fear, because a growling voice entered my mind.

~*We're going to be okay, Vega. You and I have been through worse together.*

"Worse than a huge army of bears and wolves?" I asked, trying and failing to inject levity into my voice.

~*We have Callum and Caffall. We have Merriwether and the Witches of many Covens. And don't forget, we have you.*

"And you. I just wish we had Dachmal and the other dragons. If ever we needed them, today is the day." A lump formed in my throat as I recalled what I'd seen in the Orb. "I wish I knew where they were. I just hope they're not…"

~*They're not with the queen,* Lachlan's drake-voice interrupted.

I can feel them out there somewhere. I don't know how to describe it, but I know they're safe. So have faith, Vega. I promise—we'll get through this.

"If only you knew how much I wanted—needed—to believe that," I lamented, watching Caffall swoop low, protectively positioning himself between the enemy's troops and our own as the Academy's former students began to emerge from the portal.

The queen's forces halted in their tracks, a mere few hundred feet away. And as the red-clad Zerkers began to position themselves in a defensive row, I could feel their nervousness on the air.

I wasn't sure I'd ever seen a frightened Zerker, and it didn't bode well for our chances of success.

~*Believe it,* Lachlan said, and I could tell he sensed the tension that had just overtaken me. *I betrayed you once—I will never do it again. Not even by lying to make you feel better.*

"Thank you, Lachlan. I really do appreciate it."

We flew some distance before we found ourselves approaching the portal, a strange, glowing circle of bluish light. Our troops were still piling out, spreading themselves out in a broad frontline, probably hoping to convince the enemy there were more of us than they knew.

But my heart sank again when the last of them appeared. I could see at last how pathetic our numbers really were when compared to those of our foes.

When I saw Merriwether emerge from the portal at long last, I laid a hand on the hilt of the Sword of Viviane, telling myself that if my gray-haired grandfather could be so brave as to step out before such a monstrous army without armor or weapons, I could surely find a small dose of courage.

"Take me down, Lachlan," I said. "Please. I want to be with Merriwether when it begins."

I felt the drake tighten below me, but he relented, knowing if he didn't bring me down himself, I would travel the distance on my own.

The Witches, led by Solara, were still airborne, and my hope increased dramatically when I saw that others had begun to join them in droves—Covens from all over the Otherwhere had begun to gather in the sky just below a dark cover of low-lying clouds.

From a distance, the Witches resembled a flock of menacing birds, and my heart soared to watch them gather like their own dark cloud looming high above the enemy.

They were more experienced warriors than any Zerker, fired up as they were after Clio's death at the hands of the Lightsmith.

The Covens had a vested interest in the outcome of this battle —and I knew without question that Solara would lead them to victory if she possibly could.

~See? Lachlan said. *We have allies everywhere. Lots of them. We just need to know where to look.*

It seemed Lachlan and I weren't the only ones invigorated by the Witches' arrival. Even from a distance, I could see how restless the Zerkers were now, eager to sink swords and axes into Ursals and Waergs.

Their shoulders were drawn back, their heads held high. It was as if the capacity for fear had suddenly been swiped from each of their minds—and I wondered for a fleeting moment if Merriwether had cast a spell of courage over our entire army.

"They're absolutely mad to want to fight those bears," I said. "But I guess I should be thankful for it."

~Psychopathy has its perks, I guess.

Lachlan's drake landed on a patch of grass near the place where Merriwether was standing. I slipped off his back, a hand landing on his neck.

"Keep your distance from the Ursals," I told him. "Use your fire to take them down or scatter them. In the meantime, I'll do what I can to defend our troops with protective spells. I just wish

I could do more. I wish...I wish there were more fighters on our side."

~Others will come, Lachlan assured me. *I heard Solara say the Rangers were traveling this way in droves, as well as Grells.*

"But where are they?" I asked, my eyes darting around, quickly scanning the horizon. "If they don't come soon..."

~Have faith, my friend. Help is on its way. I promise. With that, Lachlan took off into the air once again.

I watched for a minute as he joined Lily. Her hand landed on his scaled neck and, nodding, she said something to him, though I had no idea what.

A bittersweet emotion flooded me. I hoped above almost everything that the two of them would find their way to lasting happiness after the battle was at an end.

As I watched, Lily spoke again, then called out to Solara, who flew toward them, then gestured dismissively with her hand. Lily slipped onto Lachlan's back, and they took off to fly north, away from the battleground.

Away from danger.

"Where the hell are they going?" I asked out loud.

Were they afraid they might not make it through the day? Was Lachlan just offering reassuring words to calm me until he could make his escape?

Could I blame him?

Still, just a minute ago, he had told me to trust him.

How was I supposed to trust someone who had left me—left *all* of us—to fight an impossible battle without his help?

"If young Lachlan is leaving, he has his reasons." A low voice spoke the words from just behind me. "But right now, we have other important matters to consider. I'm afraid I need you to focus, Vega, my dear."

I spun around to see Merriwether, his eyes trained on a distant point—one that lay well beyond the Ursals and Waergs.

I followed his gaze to see two figures astride large horses, positioned like proud statues on top of a hill.

They were hundreds of feet from us, yet I knew exactly who they were.

The Usurper Queen and her awful husband Lumus...keeping a safe distance from potential harm.

31
WAR

I WAS ALMOST SURPRISED TO SEE THAT LUMUS HADN'T SHIFTED into some form other than human—but then, I didn't suppose he or his traitorous wife intended to fight.

Better to have their servants risk their lives while they stay out of harm's way.

Except that they *weren't* out of harm's way.

Because soaring through the sky above us all was a beautiful golden dragon who was probably itching to barbecue them where they stood—not to mention hundreds of Witches.

"Someone should kill the queen and that bastard right now," I growled. "Solara could—"

Merriwether interrupted me with a raised hand. "Lumus and Isla wouldn't have come if they'd feared for a second that it might mean their end. The warlock has tricks up his sleeve. Right now, he and Isla are comfortably seated behind a powerful protective shield that will only lower if one of them chooses to cast an offensive spell—and as you know, his spells are often deadly. As much as it pains me to say it, Solara is wise to keep her Sisters away from him—particularly after what happened with the Lightsmith."

I looked up to see the Witches hovering in formation, waiting for the moment the battle began. But Merriwether was right. Not one of them seemed to have their sights set on Lumus or the queen.

Something occurred to me then.

"Where's Raff?" I asked. "Where's their jackass of a son?"

"Word has it," Merriwether replied, "that Raff has fled with a small contingent of Waergs into the mountains."

"So he's hiding like a coward instead of fighting," I muttered. "Figures."

Quiet disappointment settled inside me. I'd never had an opportunity to get my revenge for all that Raff put the other Seekers and me through all those months ago.

I didn't exactly relish the thought of hurting anyone, and I wasn't a person consumed by bloodlust.

But for him, I might have made an exception.

My eyes moved again to Solara, who hovered at the forefront of the enormous flock of Witches. As if she could hear our conversation, her eyes locked on the queen and Lumus, and I could tell that she was calculating her chances of success if she should try to cast a spell or two in their direction.

Silently, I reached out to her, hoping to connect our minds as I'd so often connected with others.

Can you hear me, Solara? I asked.

But when no reply came, I refocused my attention on the miles of enemies in the distance.

The Ursals stood with their heads low, lips pulled back in threatening snarls. The creatures were so large they had no need of armor—which was probably a good thing, as it would have taken all the metal in the Otherwhere to cover them.

It would take many arrows, I mused, *to kill even one of them.*

There weren't enough arrows in all the Academy's arsenal to begin to take even half of them down. For all their training and all their energy, I couldn't imagine the Zerkers or Rangers in our ranks doing much damage to any of the massive bears.

Solara came swooping down toward the road, landing gently next to me. Merriwether had stepped away to give last-minute words of wisdom to some of the troops, his eyes moving occasionally to Callum, then back to the enemy's forces.

"Where did Lachlan and Lily go?" I asked Solara. "I saw them fly north."

"Lily said they were going to see someone. When I asked who, she confessed that she didn't know."

"Who could they possibly have gone to see? Did they suddenly forget there's a war raging?"

Solara reacted as though my words stung her to the core. "I have a fear in my heart," she said. "After what happened between you and Lachlan—after he tried to hurt you under Meligant's influence—I worry that he's run off to keep himself away from all of this."

Solara was Lachlan's aunt, and I understood her sympathy for him. But if that was his reason for leaving, then he was as much of a coward as Raff.

He had seemed so confident a few minutes ago—so certain we could win.

Why had he deserted us in the face of everything he knew we were up against?

"You really think he's afraid of what he might do?"

Solara shook her head, worry in her eyes. "The truth is, I don't know. Lachlan has never fully opened up to me about his trauma. He went through so much, Vega, and it nearly destroyed him. I can only hope he's managed to talk to Lily about it."

Any unkind thoughts in my mind faded in that moment, and I scolded myself, resolving to support my friend.

Lachlan was no coward, and no weakling. He had protected me so many times and risked life and limb to keep me alive. There had to be more to it than desertion.

"Solara, I know him so well, and I can't imagine him shying away from this day—from this battle. He cares too much about the outcome. He told me he'd do anything he could to support Callum's claim to the throne. I just—I don't get it."

"Then tell me, Vega—where did he go?"

I pulled my eyes to the enemy again, my jaw clenched. "I don't know. I wish I did, but I—"

A horn blared through the air, and our troops froze in place, their posture suddenly ramrod straight.

Seeming to understand the significance of this moment, Solara shot into the air to join the other Witches.

My knees trembled as my gaze fell on the Ursals' soulless eyes, which seemed so close now that I could see the various colors in their irises, the stains on their fangs, the subtleties of their fur.

War was upon us. There was no stopping it now.

I inhaled a long, final calming breath as Callum's deep voice cut through the air.

"My allies! Rangers, Zerkers, Casters, Witches, and Wizards!" he shouted. "The battle is about to begin! With it, the fate of the Otherwhere will be determined. We have no choice but to win—and win we will!"

Rows of Rangers and Zerkers, some of them armed with longbows, shouted approving cries of, "Yes, we will!" and "Long live our Future King!"

The shouts rose up, crescendoing through the air until they were deafening. I was more grateful than I could say for the chorus of Zerkers itching for a fight. Their courage added itself to my own, and I could only hope it would be enough.

As much as the Zerkers had irritated me when we'd trained at the Academy, it was impossible now not to admire them at least a little. They were fearless and brave in the face of the coming mission. They knew perfectly well that they might die.

In fact, death had begun to seem extremely likely.

Yet they loved the Otherwhere so much that they were willing to die so that others might have a beautiful future.

That alone was one of the most noble sentiments I could possibly imagine.

Merriwether stepped over to me and took me by the shoulders. "Vega—if I ask it of you, I need you to summon the Lyre of Adair immediately."

"Of course. But—are you going to play it?"

"Me?" he said, offering up a wink. "Not a chance. But I happen to know a player who is very talented—one we will summon too, when the time comes. But for now, it's time to do battle."

He stepped away and I pulled my eyes to Callum and Caffall. The dragon, with his eyes locked on the queen and Lumus, let out a cry that sliced through the sky like a blade.

If ever a signal had called for war, that was it.

32
IT BEGINS

When they heard Caffall's cry, the Ursals, panicked, began to charge.

Some ran for the surrounding hills and woods, tearing themselves away from the battleground. Most, though, set their sights on our troops, as they'd been trained to do.

The earth shook below my feet when they crashed toward us on enormous paws, horrific bellows and growls erupting from their open, fang-filled mouths.

"Archers, prepare, then fire at will!" Callum commanded, his voice echoing against the surrounding hills.

The Rangers, positioned as they were behind the Zerkers, nocked and fired, unleashing an arcing barrage of razor-sharp arrows at the enemy's front line.

Some of the Ursals stumbled, and a few of them even fell.

But most gathered themselves and continued to rampage toward us despite the many arrows jutting out from their flesh.

Seeing that our troops were about to be trampled, Caffall dove down, letting loose a long, brutal stream of flame that cut across the landscape to create a wall of fire between us and our foes.

"A warning," I said under my breath.

Caffall could have taken out a hundred Ursals, but Callum wasn't cruel, and neither was the dragon. Neither had the heart to burn the enemy alive unless they had no other choice.

Many of the Ursals, seeing the fire, fled, this time out of a pure survival instinct. But even after I'd watched forty or more of them disappear into the distance, their numbers still managed to seem insurmountable.

The Rangers shot another mass of arrows while the Zerkers, just beyond Caffall's wall of fire, drew their melee weapons, preparing for the worst.

Banking and swooping back around, Caffall flew at the bears once again. Their pace was not slowing, despite the licking flame, and within seconds they would be on our troops.

Callum issued a command to Caffall, who dove down again. This time, he hurled a series of fireballs at the Ursals on the frontlines. Flame engulfed the creatures, their horrid screams filling the air.

Many of the bears—forty or fifty—fell to their painful deaths, and in spite of myself, my heart hurt for them.

"Tools of a cruel queen," Merriwether said with pain in his voice. "Poor creatures. They were meant to live in the wild, where they belong."

I knew full well that Callum, too, must be hurting. It wasn't in his nature to kill, and certainly not to kill animals. But the Ursals had given him little choice.

Still, beyond the fallen bears were many, many more of their kind—and it was time for our army to spring into action.

I summoned a small contingent of Flame-Warriors to stand before the Zerkers, bows or swords in hand and ready to fight the queen's forces. The Ursals, meanwhile, kept coming, leaping over their fallen allies and closing the gap between themselves and our frontline.

As they advanced, so did the black cloud of Witches above us, who dove down in a synchronized movement, hurling destructive spells at the encroaching force as they went.

Some cast ice spells, others fire, lightning, or even conjured shards of what looked like glass, which embedded itself in the creatures' sides, necks, and heads.

But still, most of the Ursals managed to run on, the earth under their paws flying up in an explosion of detritus.

My Flame-Warriors were the first on the ground to collide with the Ursals, the bears' sharp fangs trying in vain to tear them apart as Merriwether and other Casters hurled a barrage of spells at the bears and the Waergs, who had moved up to join them in the attack.

My summoned forces fought until the last of their embers had sputtered and faded, and then, it was a mere matter of seconds before the sickening sound of colliding bodies met my ears.

Inhuman cries rang through the air as bears tore at the flesh of Zerkers and Rangers, and nausea overtook me as I tried and failed to focus.

Vega. You need to help. It's what you do.

With adrenaline fueling me, I leapt forward, summoning a series of dense, transparent shields to protect our forces. The barriers hovered and moved with each of our warriors, blocking swipes from the animals' fierce claws—yet allowing the Zerkers enough space to swing their weapons.

For a little while, it seemed that my plan was succeeding. Ursal after Ursal fell as the Zerkers managed to slip under their shields and slice the creatures' legs or ram weapons into their chests before retreating behind the safety of the barriers.

But the bears' numbers were too great, and for each one that fell, it seemed that five more appeared.

"There are too many of them!" I cried as I tried and failed to summon enough shields to keep our soldiers alive. One after the other, I watched as Zerkers tumbled to the ground, bloodied and beaten by the Ursals' sword-like talons.

By now, Callum and Caffall were high in the air again. The dragon couldn't afford to send flame hurtling toward the battleground for fear of taking out half our troops.

We need the Northern Rangers! I called out silently to Callum. *The Grells! Where are our allies?*

As if in answer, somewhere in the distance, a cry rang out.

This one didn't come from a dragon or from a Waerg or from a bear.

It was the cry of a Grell—a battle cry, calling out to let us know they had come, and that they would fight alongside us until the end.

When I spotted them cresting a nearby hill, my heart sang. Clad in specially designed leather boots and armor, they charged. Their horns were as effective a weapon as any sword, and they moved like wild creatures, unafraid of the deadliest foe.

At the head of their army was Kohrin Icewalker, the first Grell I'd ever met—a loyal ally to the Academy.

But even as they sprinted toward us on their powerful hooves, I cried out.

"They're passing too close to Lumus and the queen! He'll kill them!"

Merriwether was at my side in an instant, his brow beading with sweat, his breath heavy in his chest. "Damn it," he growled.

Already, we could see Lumus turning his mount to face the incoming force. His horse, uneasy when he saw such a mass of springing creatures, froze in place as if the warlock had paralyzed him.

Lumus lifted his hands in the air, fingers splayed to shoot a destructive spell toward our allies. It was like an invisible bomb had gone off, sending a shockwave through the air that knocked most of the Grells instantly to the ground.

Some failed to stir after that, and I knew without asking that they were dead.

I watched as Kohrin rose to his feet and without missing a beat, he continued to lead the charge.

Lumus, it seemed, found such determination unbearable. He aimed his sights on Kohrin, preparing to shoot off another spell.

"Caffall!" I cried, fearing that the worst was about to happen.

~*I see him*, the dragon replied, sweeping down, Callum's eyes laser-focused on Lumus.

Merriwether had said the protective shield around him and Isla would fail if he shot out an offensive spell, which meant he was probably vulnerable right now.

This was Caffall's chance to take him down at long last.

The dragon hurled a bolt of flame at Lumus, narrowly missing him as the warlock's mount took off, galloping in the other direction before spinning around and shooting something toward the dragon.

But instead of a spell, it looked like some kind of projectile—a harpoon of some sort, perhaps. Except this wasn't like any harpoon I'd ever seen.

For one thing, it had wings.

It flew through the air in a strange, disorderly way, veering this way and that, but consistently aiming itself at the dragon.

"What *is* that thing?" I asked Merriwether.

"A raven-spear," my grandfather replied. "A charmed weapon controlled by the caster's mind. It will keep flying until it reaches its target, unless someone manages to catch and destroy it."

With dismay settling inside me, I saw that he was right. As much as Caffall banked and weaved, he was unable to lose the weapon, which finally grazed his chest before banking in the air to aim for him once again.

"Can't you stop it?" I cried, terrified for Caffall and Callum both.

"It's too far away," he replied, "but the Witches are trying their best." He pointed to the sky where Solara and a few others were already in pursuit of the weapon.

Solara moved fast, a mere blur in the sky as she drew her sword and pursued the spear, almost catching up to it once or twice before it managed to veer away in an irritating evasive maneuver.

One of her fellow Witches came at it from another direction, and for a moment, I was convinced that they had it.

But the raven-spear slipped between them and once again went after Caffall, who was flying north now, trying to draw the weapon toward a dense forest of tall trees.

"Come on, Callum," I whispered, my heart beating so hard it somehow seemed louder than the cries of the hundreds of fighters in the distance.

Solara was after the weapon again, as were six or seven other Witches, hands grasping, spells flying, in desperate attempts to bring it down.

But they were too slow. The spear accelerated to a blinding speed and found its mark, tearing viciously into Caffall's left wing.

A cry of agony cut through the air and froze my blood.

I watched as Caffall tumbled toward the earth with Callum clinging desperately to his neck...

And I watched as the golden dragon crashed, full speed, into the ground.

33
WAR WOUNDS

THE COLLISION WAS SICKENING, AND AT FIRST, I WAS TERRIFIED that both Caffall and Callum were dead.

I sprinted toward them, crying out for Niala and Rourke. "We need you!" I screamed, desperate to reach Callum.

When I saw him leaping off the dragon and Caffall's head rising weakly, temporary relief flooded me. But I could see that Caffall, though alive, was badly wounded.

As I ran, I pulled my eyes to the sky to see that Solara had grabbed hold of the raven-spear. She took it in both hands and snapped it in half like a twig, her face a display of pure rage.

Niala was at my side a moment later, with Rourke darting up ahead in panther form.

I glared over to where the queen and Lumus still sat on their horses, arrogant expressions on their awful faces.

I wanted to scream at them. "You failed! They're still alive!" but the last thing I wanted was tempt Lumus to do further damage.

Instead, I threw a hand up to create a temporary transparent wall between us and a roof high overhead—one that would protect Caffall and Callum from further attacks.

"Are you all right?" I asked as I reached Callum, throwing myself into his arms.

"I'm okay," he replied, pulling back, his eyes moving to Niala. "You can heal him, can't you?"

She nodded, breathless. "I can," she said. "It's not a terrible wound—it's just the membrane. I'll have him as good as new before you know it, I promise. Just give me a few minutes."

Callum looked beyond relieved.

"I didn't know Lumus could summon weaponry like that," I began to say, but Merriwether, who had just joined our small party, shook his head.

"It wasn't entirely his doing. The raven-spear was summoned by the Usurper Queen."

I stared at him. "The queen?" I asked. "But she can't cast like that. She's no Witch."

"I got a good look at her when the spear pursued Caffall. She's wearing a ring of Deep Magic—a piece I've seen before, many years ago. One that was stolen from none other than Morgan Le Fay. That ring is imbued with magic that would make your blood freeze—and until we take it from her, I'm afraid we have little chance in this war. That ring," he added, turning to face the queen and Lumus, blurry through my conjured wall, "could be the key to her mastery of the Ursals. I suspect that without it they would turn on her, in fact—or flee to their homes in the wild."

"Then we have to take it!" Callum cried, leaping around my barrier, his sword drawn. "Enough of this ridiculous war! Too many lives have already been lost. It's time my sister paid the price for what she's done."

"Mr. Drake!" Merriwether shouted, but Callum's rage at the injury inflicted on Caffall was far too great, and there was no stopping him. "Do not do this!"

Merriwether darted after him and I followed, leaving Niala and Rourke to tend to Caffall.

I knew what my grandfather had to be thinking. As powerful

as Callum was, as adept a melee fighter, he and a mere short sword were no match for a warlock and a ring of Deep Magic.

Watching Callum approach, Lumus positioned his horse before the queen, a smile on his lips.

"It was far too easy to summon you to me, Mr. Drake," Lumus shouted. "You're more foolish than I thought."

"You're an arrogant ass, Lumus. I should have taken you on years ago," Callum snarled.

"Taken me on? I would love to see you try—genuinely," Lumus retorted. And with that, he raised his hands in the air, conjuring a spell of putrid, greenish vapor that twisted and turned over between his palms.

Just as he readied himself to hurl it at Callum, a projectile of pure light exploded through the air, aimed squarely at the warlock's chest.

When it collided with his flesh, Lumus flew backwards off his horse, who galloped away, terrified.

A moment later, Merriwether was standing protectively between Callum and Lumus, hands fisted at his sides. I was some distance behind them, but I could hear every word they spoke as clearly as if I'd been next to them.

"You will *not* hurt the rightful heir!" Merriwether called out. "You will return to the depths, where your soul was born!"

A low, diabolical laugh rose up in Lumus's throat, his eyes flaring bright.

"The rightful heir does not always gain a seat on the throne, or have you never read a history book, Merriwether?" he snarled, conjuring another spiraling spell between his palms.

The warlock raised his hands, set to cast his violent spell.

"Grandfather!" I cried.

"I see him, Vega," Merriwether's voice assured me. "I see him."

But in the end, it was the queen herself who took my grandfather down.

34

LOSS

The green stones of the stolen ring glowed on Isla's finger when she threw her hands into the air and called upon some ancient incantation—one that had no business crossing her lips.

She was no Sorcière. She was a jealous wanna-be and nothing more. An imposter in the world of magic users—one who had never cast a spell without stealing from someone else.

But in the end, it didn't matter. Stolen magic or not, her spell turned out to be devastatingly effective.

A hail of daggers flew at Merriwether, who instantly hurled a counter-spell to stop them in mid-air. When his magic met the weapons, most of them fell uselessly to the ground.

But one of the blades struck him square in the chest.

He fell to his knees, then collapsed to the ground, his body limp.

With a scream I ran to him, hurling my hands toward the queen and her husband. Fire shot from my fingers—long streams of raging blue flame exploding in their direction.

One of the bolts caught Lumus off-guard, searing his left arm and drawing a cry from his lips.

"I'll kill you!" I screamed. "I will take both of you down, so help me!"

I shot another spell at them, and another and another, fireballs flying through the air and landing mere inches from Lumus's feet as he turned and fled, leaping onto Isla's mount behind her.

They galloped into the distance, disappearing through a transparent portal that sealed up instantly behind them.

"Cowards!" I screamed as Callum caught hold of me. "Monsters!"

He wrapped his arms tight around me, holding me to his chest, his breath in my ear.

"It's okay," he said softly. "It will be okay."

I didn't believe him. How could anything ever be okay again?

Pulling free, I sprinted to the place where my grandfather lay, the blade still stuck in his chest.

"Niala!" I cried.

The last thing I wanted was to tear her away from Caffall if she wasn't finished healing his wing. But Caffall's wound wasn't life-threatening.

I wasn't so sure about my grandfather's.

I reached for the blade embedded in Merriwether's chest, but he shook his head. "Don't," he said weakly.

"But..."

"Niala will help me if she can. Vega...it's time. Summon the Lyre. When that is done, then you and Callum can finally finish what you've begun."

"But we can't. Not without you," I murmured, tears streaming down my cheeks. "We need you."

"Trust me one last time, Granddaughter," he said with a weak smile. "Call the Lyre, and call its player to these lands."

"Who is the player?"

"A certain woman," he rasped, his breath coming in short

bursts, "with a set of lovely eyes set on an intelligent face. One we both love dearly, you…and…I."

My heart hammered in my chest. No—he couldn't possibly mean…

"You want me to summon Nana?"

He nodded, his eyes closing. "Quickly, now."

Niala was with him a moment later, kneeling down, fighting back tears as we all were. Pressing her hands to his chest to either side of the dagger, she began to recite a healing incantation.

I rose to my feet and pulled my eyes to the sky. The clouds were parting, and evening was about to fall. The distant sun had turned a deep red and loomed heavy over the horizon.

"The sun has turned to blood," I whispered, recalling the words my grandfather had said to me not long ago.

"When war storms its way through the Otherwhere and the sun turns to blood, the Player shall arrive and strum the tune that will wake the mightiest force this land has ever known."

With that, I summoned the Lyre of Adair, which appeared instantly in my hands.

Now, all I had to do was call forth its player.

I slammed my eyes shut and, with every bit of strength inside me, called out to my grandmother.

You haven't been here in a long time—and you probably thought you'd never come here again. But we need you, Nana…Merriwether needs you. Please, come.

She had once been a Seeker, like me. She'd been chosen from a field of competitors to find the Relics, just as I had.

The only difference was that Nana had done it alone.

She was the bravest, strongest woman I'd ever met.

I only hoped her strength would be enough to get her through the next few minutes.

"I'm here." The voice that spoke the two simple words was so familiar—yet somehow, it felt like a stranger's voice.

When I opened my eyes, the woman who stood before me

was around my height, her hair a tangle of silver waves. She looked like my Nana, but somehow different at the same time.

She seemed younger and more vibrant, her eyes bright and determined.

If I hadn't already known it, it would have been impossible to guess her age—probably because it lay somewhere between the seventeen-year-old version of herself who had once spent time in the Otherwhere and the older version I knew so well.

She had become timeless, ethereal. *Miraculous.*

She smiled at me, then, when her gaze landed on Merriwether, something crossed her face—a pang of regret, of sorrow.

His eyes opened and landed on her face, and untold years of lost conversations passed between them in an instant.

For the briefest moment, I almost forget about the battle raging so close by.

"Mer," Nana said softly, using the nickname I had only ever heard the Lightsmith use. "Are you going to be all right?"

"You're here at last," he replied weakly. "So of course I will."

Turning back to me, Nana cleared her throat. "We have no time to waste, I'm afraid. No time to reacquaint ourselves. There's a battle to win."

"You know why you're here?" I breathed.

She nodded. "I've always known I would be back eventually. This place has called to me before, but never so desperately as now." Extending her hands, she added, "The Lyre, Vega."

Screams and wails sounded in the near distance, but all I could hear was Nana's voice. My eyes were locked on her face—on the woman she once was in those years long before I was born—and I knew something momentous was about to occur.

Time itself had shifted and ebbed—and the world itself had changed.

I handed her the golden instrument, and she held it to her chest.

"Callum Drake," she said, turning his way. "It's time you met your ancestor at long last. He's an impressive fellow, to say the least."

Callum took me by the hand and held on tight. "I look forward to his arrival," he said.

It seemed everyone but me knew what was about to happen.

Nana closed her eyes and plucked at the strings. A beautiful, sweet music wafted through the air, drowning out all the pain and torment around us.

I watched her, trying not to panic as my gaze moved to the place where Caffall had crashed to the ground. His head was up now, and he managed to rise to his feet, seemingly awaiting the stranger's arrival, just as the rest of us were.

Callum stood by, his eyes locked on the battle. I knew without a word that he was aching to fight—that under any other circumstances, he would have picked up a weapon and attacked every one of the enemy's soldiers until the bitter end.

But he would not leave Caffall or Merriwether—not until he knew they were safe.

Nana kept caressing the Lyre's strings, her eyes closed, her expression peaceful and distant, almost as though she weren't standing on the edge of a bloody war.

Moving closer to Callum, I was hesitant when I asked, "What exactly will happen when she finishes playing?"

"Something that hasn't happened in many, many years." Callum replied, his eyes pulling to the distant hills. "The Pendragon will rise again."

35
THE LYRE OF ADAIR

OUR FIGHTERS WERE STILL CLASHING WITH THE ENEMY FORCES AS Nana played.

The Zerkers among our ranks had quickly discovered that the best way to vanquish the Ursals was to leap onto their backs and assault them from above while the Rangers fired carefully-timed barrages of precisely aimed arrows.

The attacks took some doing—not to mention the kind of bravery only an arrogant fool could muster.

Thank God Zerkers are so foolish.

The Casters flung spell after spell at the enemy, temporarily disorienting the giant beasts while fighting off encroaching Waergs.

Most of the multitude of Witches were still airborne, though some had been taken down by the queen's archers hidden among the Waergs' numbers.

Solara shouted commands from above, taking control over the magical contingent of our army. I had never been more grateful for her level-headed leadership than I was at that moment—nor had I ever been prouder to know her.

The Grells, too, fought with extraordinary courage, their

strength almost as great as the Waergs'. Though they lacked fangs and claws, their hooves and horns made for impressive weapons, and they fought with a ferocity I didn't know they were capable of.

I didn't think it was possible for my heart to beat any faster than it already was.

But as my mind slowly registered the words Callum had uttered, I began to feel like my chest might actually explode.

The Pendragon will rise again.

Did he mean what I thought he did? Could it possibly be…

When Nana finished playing, she set the Lyre on the ground. The moment it touched the earth, it vanished.

A whimper escaped my lips to realize another Relic of Power was gone.

"It's all right, Vega," Nana said, her voice soothing. "The Lyre simply knows its mission is complete."

"But nothing has happened!" I protested.

"Hasn't it?" Stepping over to Merriwether, she knelt and laid a hand on his cheek. As if they knew something I failed to understand, they both turned to stare at the tallest hill in the distance.

Callum slipped over to my side and took my hand, and through his touch, I felt a surge of confidence.

"I don't understand what's happening," I whispered.

"The battle will end soon," he replied, "and then you and I have only one last fight to win."

"One last fight, then you will be king," I said.

"All that matters is that the Usurper Queen will be taken down. This battle isn't for my glory, but for the good of the lands around us. This is a fight for the Otherwhere—and it's one we have to win."

I didn't know what I was expecting to see on the hill, exactly—I only knew that hope was easing its way through my bloodstream for the first time in what felt like hours.

Despite the mounds of dead and wounded fighters who lay on

the mud-field where the battle was still raging, optimism found its way to my heart as I felt a surge of power on the air.

Something magical was about to occur—something that had been coming for centuries.

The blood-sun faded, turning golden once more on the horizon as silver-clad figures began to appear at the crest of the tall hill.

There were many of them—a hundred, at least. Some rode horses, others strode along the ground. At the small army's center was one who shone brighter than the others, his armor glowing gold as it picked up the sun's rays.

By now, those who were still doing battle had noticed the newcomers and had frozen in place as if they, too, felt the mysterious power on the air.

To my surprise, the tall figure moved swiftly toward our small party rather than toward the battlefield. His army, on the other hand, stormed its way toward the mud-caked fighters, unleashing battle cries unlike any sound I had ever heard.

Merriwether, his voice still frail even after Niala's healing, said, "Vega—you have kept the Sword of Viviane safe, but now it's time to give it to its wielder."

I stepped forward with Callum at my side, daunted by the strange, almost ghostly entity who was moving toward us as though he were lighter than air.

Callum's eyes were locked on the man, even more awestruck than I was.

As we neared the stranger, I pulled the Sword of Viviane from its sheath and held it out.

The man stopped before me, his chin high. His hair was ash blond and curly, his beard neatly trimmed.

But what was most striking about him was that his eyes were the same piercing blue as Callum's.

He glanced over toward Caffall, then at Callum, and said,

"The Pendragon's heir will soon take back the throne, and we are here to aid him. Let us finish this battle while *you* finish the war."

Holy. Crap.

"You're really..." I said, my voice catching. "Arthur Pendragon?"

He nodded, taking the sword that was sometimes called Excalibur, grasping its hilt in both fists. "I am," he said, glancing over his shoulder to the field where his companions were already clashing with Ursals, Waergs, and other enemy forces. "And my knights have come for this, the last battle. We will herd the Ursals back to the wilds of this land—and we will ensure that no traitorous Waerg is left standing."

"Those are the knights...of the Round Table?" I replied, looking over at the fearless force. "I didn't know there were so many."

"One-hundred-and-fifty," Callum said as though repeating a fact he'd learned in history class.

"That's right," King Arthur replied, bowing his head. "May you one day soon have so many loyal allies to support you." He slid a hand over the side of the sword's blade, smiling as his eyes landed on its gleaming silver. "Hello, old friend."

I had no idea what to say, so I just nodded, my jaw slack.

He pulled his gaze back to mine. "The sword will return to you when the time comes to use it, Daughter of Viviane."

Pivoting away from us, the king, who had once ruled over Britain, let out a war cry, then charged toward the battle, tearing our enemies down with shocking ease as our tired soldiers backed away, as stunned as I was.

"Are he and his knights...are they...?" I half-whispered, unsure of how to phrase the question.

"Dead?" Callum replied. "No. The old legends say they dwell eternally in another place—somewhere far from here. Somewhere we may one day get to visit, Vega. A beautiful realm, where the Knights of the Round Table and their kin have earned their place for eternity."

They're immortal, I thought. I supposed it was why they were so strong, so unflinchingly brave in the face of wild beasts.

As we watched, they made quick work of the enemy, driving the Ursals back toward the woods where they had once lived in peace. The bears were willing enough to fight Zerkers, but their sense of self-preservation kicked in when it came to an immortal army threatening to tear them to shreds with magic-imbued weaponry.

Some of the remaining Waergs were foolish enough to stay and fight, but most turned tail and sprinted after the Ursals, disappearing into the distant woods.

As promised, Arthur's knights pursued them, gaining on them easily and cutting them down for their treachery.

I found myself pitying the creatures I had once loathed so deeply. Somewhere inside those Waergs had once been a shred of humanity—and now, they had no chance of redeeming themselves.

"Vega," Merriwether called out in his weakened voice.

I stepped over to crouch by his side, taking his hand in mine. "Yes, Grandfather?"

"It's time. You and Callum must strike while the queen and Lumus are vulnerable. Go to Uldrach and confront them one last time."

"Just the two of us?" I asked, panicking. There were fighters still standing, and the battle was nearly over.

Couldn't we take a small army with us?

"Alone," he said with a nod of his head. "I've watched this night play out in the Orb of Kilarin. I know what must be done—and you will see it soon enough." When he sensed my growing apprehension, he added, "As the Pendragon reminded you, you are a Daughter of Viviane. Callum is a son of the Pendragon.

Never were two beings so well-qualified to do battle for this realm. Don't be afraid, my dear."

Unfortunately, the words *Don't be afraid* were far more easily spoken than accomplished. After all, Dachmal and the other dragons were still unaccounted for—and for all I knew, the queen and Lumus had imprisoned them in Uldrach again.

They were probably lying in wait for Callum's and my arrival, anticipating the moment when they could force the beasts to unleash a furious stream of flame in our direction.

"Ask the Orb, Vega," Merriwether said, reading my expression as expertly as ever. "It will answer your question."

Wincing, I summoned the Orb of Kilarin and watched the smoke at its center clear as I asked, "Where is Dachmal?"

I saw the blue dragon then, soaring through the evening sky. Behind him was Tefyr, his silver companion.

On Dachmal's back was a lone rider. But on Tefyr, for some reason, there were *two* riders.

"The queen, Lumus, and Raff, making an escape?" I asked, but the more I stared at the silhouettes, the more I knew they couldn't be those three. For one thing, the dragons were flying south over the mountains—if anything, they were headed *toward* Uldrach, not away from it.

"Go," Merriwether said, sitting up for the first time and taking Nana's hand in his while he crafted a portal with his other hand. Ten or so feet from us, it swirled open to reveal Uldrach's dark interior.

The last place in the Otherwhere I wished to go.

"Callum," my grandfather called, "You know what I'm about to tell you, don't you?"

Callum nodded gravely. "Caffall can't come," he said.

"His wound is healing, but he needs more time. Flying at this point is out of the question. But you won't need the golden dragon—not where you're going. Use your wits, and remember, do not be afraid. We will see each other again very soon."

Callum nodded. Then, taking my hand in his, he led me through the portal and into our destiny.

36
ULDRACH

The moment Callum and I stepped through the portal, it sealed shut, reminding us that we were now completely on our own.

We found ourselves in a broad corridor of dark stone, the hulking silhouettes of ancient statues lining the walls to either side. They were meant to represent men—brave ancestors of the Crimson King who had once done battle in these lands—but in the shadows, they felt more like slouching gargoyles glaring at us from behind dead eyes.

I knew I could bring Callum to the safety of the Academy if I should need to—but a voice deep in my soul told me not to think about escape.

Not before our final battle was won.

"We can't leave," Callum said, reading my mind as we moved tentatively forward. "Tonight, the fate of the Otherwhere will be determined—and it's up to you and me to seal it."

"I know," I replied, squeezing his hand. "It's just…"

Callum stopped and turned my way, cupping my chin in his hand and lifting my eyes to his.

"Vega Sloane," he whispered. I closed my eyes, and for one

sweet moment, I was standing with him in the Novel Hovel in Fairhaven.

Sunlight poured in through the front window, highlighting dancing specks of dust, and for just a few seconds, my heart beat with excitement rather than with fear.

"I love you," Callum said, "more than anything. And I believe in you. I have *always* believed in you, from the very first. You were chosen to come to the Otherwhere to fight for its survival—and, reluctant and frightened though you were, you did it. You fought your way to this very moment, through loss and pain. You gave everything you had, all in the hopes that this land could one day thrive. Do not let my cruel sister and her warlock husband / partner put an end to your courage. They do not deserve to break you. And they sure as hell aren't going to break me."

I nodded and opened my eyes, and the beautiful scene around us faded once again to shadow. "I won't. I promise," I said, then kissed him. But before we moved on, I added, "I need you to promise me something, too."

"Anything."

Tears burned my eyes, my lip trembling as I mustered the courage to utter the words. "Promise me you'll tell Will and Liv that I love them."

Callum chuckled, shaking his head. "I won't promise any such thing."

My brows met, my tears halting in their tracks. "What do you mean? Why not?"

"Because nothing is going to happen to you. Not tonight—not ever. Do you hear me? Whatever tricks Isla and Lumus have up their sleeves, they lack the two things you and I have on our side."

At that, I managed to smile. "What would those two things be?"

"Hope for a better future...and a love that will not be cut down by any sword or spell."

My chest heated at those words. I wanted to hold him, to stay here for an hour, absorbing his strength.

But it was time to move.

"Fine," I said, kissing him quickly. "I'll tell Will and Liv I love them myself."

"That's my girl."

Callum put an arm around me, and we advanced toward Uldrach's Throne Room until Isla's echoing voice met our ears.

"Welcome, my beloved guests!"

I reached instinctively to my side to see if the Sword of Viviane had reappeared, but no hilt met my hand.

I had no weapon at my disposal, other than my wits.

I'm so dead.

I half expected the Throne Room to be teeming with Waergs or even Ursals. But instead, as we slipped through its open doors, we saw that it was almost empty. The echoing chamber was rendered more cavernous and daunting than usual by the sky's looming darkness and by the faint glow of the moon, barely visible through a stained glass window.

Isla sat in the throne, a lone figure slouched back casually as her eyes landed on us from the shadows. The green gems on her ring reflected the chamber's meager light, a terrible, rage-inspiring reminder of what she had done to Caffall and Merriwether.

But where is Lumus?

"Brother," a silken voice sang, the word slithering along the walls as it made its way to our ears. "How nice to see you back at home."

"Uldrach was *never* home to me," Callum growled. "But you know that, don't you, Sister?"

He stalked toward her as I hung back, apprehensive. Lumus had to be here somewhere—I could feel his foulness on the air.

As a precaution, I conjured two flame-warriors to walk beside me as I advanced deeper into the room. The fiery figures illuminated the space so that I could see Isla's pale face reflecting the flames, her eyes dancing with my conjured fire.

"You're wondering where my dear husband is," she purred. "It's quite all right. He's...around."

"Of course he is," Callum said. "Then again, you don't need him, do you? You're powerful all on your own—as you proved when you went after my dragon."

As if in reaction to the compliment, Isla reached over and let her finger hover above the green ring. "I *am* powerful," she replied. "More powerful than you, dear brother, given that your dragon is miles away from here. Perhaps you'll regret your decision to come."

"Perhaps."

When Callum was close, the queen rose to her feet, a sudden glow emanating from her skin. Her lips were painted ruby red, her dress black and form-fitting.

She's been waiting for this moment for so long. All so she can end her brother at last. But I will never let her.

If it takes my death to keep him alive, so be it.

I spun around suddenly, my eyes desperately scanning the chamber for Lumus. When I finally spotted his glowing, silver eyes, he stepped out from the shadows, flicking a hand in the air to illuminate the Throne Room with a series of flaring torches.

The space behind him—a large alcove set deep in the side of the chamber where there had once been a caged dragon—contained a sleeping Ursal, its ribcage heaving.

It was the biggest bear I'd ever seen, its fur silver-white like that of the wolf form Lumus sometimes took on.

"His name is Bjorn," Lumus said, glancing over his shoulder at the beast. "He's a fine pet. Very obedient."

"A *pet*," I laughed. "Since when does the great and powerful Lumus need a bear for protection?"

I must have hit a nerve, because he scowled at me, then, with a rapid flick of his fingers, shot a spell in my direction.

It was a little nothing of a spell—just a weak, narrow lightning bolt—and I knew instantly that he was only doing it to test my reflexes.

I raised a hand in reaction, stopping the spell in its tracks, then turned to face Isla.

"You nearly killed my grandfather," I snarled.

"He got in the way," she replied with a shrug, then brought her eyes back to Callum's. "What I *really* wanted was to hurt my brother—which is why I'm so very glad you two came to see us."

With that, she thrust a hand out, her ring flaring bright green. A barrage of razor-sharp arrows shot toward Callum, their speed shocking.

But I was ready.

I threw a protective wall up between Callum and the barbs. The barbs pinged off of it with a rapid-fire series of sharp clangs before plunking to the ground and disappearing.

"My brother needs a woman to protect him, does he?" the Usurper Queen laughed. "I suppose it's not entirely surprising. He always *was* a pathetic thing."

I was about to snap at her when Callum spoke.

"I will gladly fight you hand-to-hand, Isla," he said calmly. "In fact, I've dreamed about it more times than I can count. Ever since you and our parents first reveled in my torture and torment, I have fantasized about repaying you for your cruelty."

"Mother and father protected you from yourself," she protested with a chuckle. "You were always destined to be a monster, and they wanted to save you from that fate! Don't you see, Brother? We did you a favor. We kept you whole as long as we could."

"You *tortured* me."

"All the more reason why you are unfit to lead this great land," Isla sneered.

"Lead?" Callum spat. "*You* would talk about leadership? All I see is a wretched, self-loathing queen standing before me. One who sent her own son away—that is, after using him for her own gains."

The mention of Raff set her on edge, a vein in her forehead bulging as her rage grew.

"Raff loves me!" she cried. "You have no right to speak of him. You're not a father—you don't understand what it is to raise a child!"

"Maybe not. But I understand better how *not* to raise one," Callum snarled. "I know what it feels like to be abused and abandoned by someone who's supposed to love you, and I suspect your son knows it, too."

The tension in the air had grown thick and oppressive. As a precaution, I kept my eyes focused on Lumus, who was slowly making his way through the room, his eyes locked on his wife.

When she offered him a quiet nod, the warlock raised a hand and flicked two fingers toward a tall door at the Throne Room's far end. It flew open to unleash a procession of ten Waergs, who leapt on large paws to the center of the chamber, teeth bared, hackles raised as they positioned themselves between Callum and me and my summoned flame-warriors still standing guard at my sides.

"You thought all our pets were on the battlefield," Isla said. "But the fun is only beginning."

37
THE LAST BATTLE

"It comes as no surprise that you continue to hide behind your wolf minions, Isla," Callum snarled as the pack of Waergs let out a chorus of growls.

"Naturally," Isla said. "It wouldn't do to ask you to fight me, as much as you long for it. It's just so...undignified. Far better to let you have it out with my furry friends."

"You don't know *how* to fight," Callum retorted, gesturing to her hand. "You only know how to harness a stolen ring to cast stolen spells."

"That's rich, coming from you, Brother. You, whose sole power lies in his bond with a dragon. Without Caffall, you're useless. Isn't that right?" She let out a laugh that rang like a set of ghastly wind chimes. "A clever ruler never lifts a blade—or a finger. Instead, she issues commands to her more...*disposable* subjects."

With those cruel words, she flicked her fingers at the Waergs —the signal to attack.

My flame-warriors spun and twisted through the air, their fiery weapons in hand, slicing down one Waerg after the other as

Callum, too, surged forward and attacked, his blade swiping at the beasts.

I hurled spell after spell, taking down one wolf then another. But each time Callum or I managed to send one crashing to the ground, another would come charging through the chamber's door.

When twenty wolves lay bloody on the Throne Room's floor, Lumus, standing in the shadows, laughed heartily, sweeping a hand through the air to make them vanish. "More!" he shouted. "Come, servants, and meet your foes!"

My chest felt like it was on the verge of caving in from exhaustion when several more wolves surged through the door.

When my flame-warriors began to fade and fizzle, I summoned four more. They surrounded me, their attacks fierce and precise. Relentless as the warriors, Callum kept swinging his sword.

"Impressive," Lumus said when we'd taken down the second wave and he had once again cleared away the evidence.

I glared at him, my chest heaving as hatred roiled inside me.

"Enough!" Callum shouted.

"I don't think it is, actually," Lumus cooed, then summoned a flock of dark shadow-birds. Smoky, distorting entities, they swooped down in coordinated attacks, their touch burning like acid when they made contact with my skin or Callum's.

I did my best to strike down the conjured entities with fireballs and other spells, summoning one after the other. But my energy was waning, my body threatening to collapse under the weight of all it had endured.

My legs were trembling from hunger and fatigue, my head swimming.

Seeing red, I spun around and hurled a bolt of flame at Lumus. He dodged it easily, vanished, and then reappeared at the far end of the chamber.

Frustrated, I summoned arrows for the flame-warriors, who

shot at the birds, dispatching them at last after several rounds of arrows.

"It's time, Isla," Callum growled, turning to the queen. "Stop this nonsense. You've known this day was coming for a long time. It's time to give in."

"Come, now," she shouted. "We haven't even gotten to the fun part yet!"

With that, she raised a hand and twisted it, gesturing toward the sleeping Ursal in the far corner.

"Callum!" I cried, spinning around to see that the bear was awake, its eyes fixed on us.

With his sword at the ready, he leapt at the bear. But even as he did, Lumus cast a spell twisting Callums's body horribly and pushing him into the air to hover high above the Throne Room's floor.

Callum's head turned unnaturally, forcing him to watch me, eyes wide.

I hurled a fireball at the bear. It collided with the bear's chest as I quickly summoned a wall between us. But the beast tore through the barrier as if it were made of paper.

Horrified, I leapt backwards, slamming into the cold stone of the chamber's wall.

Leaping toward me, the bear lifted a paw and, growling horrifically, slashed it at me. I managed to dodge once, twice... but on the third attempt, a set of blade-sharp claws slashed through my pant leg, tearing into my thigh.

I screamed in pain, crashing to my knees onto the cold stone floor.

A monstrous giant readying itself for the death blow, the bear rose up on its hind legs.

Callum, struggling against Lumus's entrapment spell, cried out desperately as he watched my final moments.

As I pulled my chin up to stare at the creature who was about to end me, only one thought worked its way through my head:

This wasn't the end Merriwether saw in the Orb.

This could not be the end for me, for Callum.

I wouldn't let it.

The Ursal's massive claws slashed toward my face, and my life flashed before my eyes. Images and scenes assaulted my mind in a rapid-fire sequence. Strangely, though, I didn't witness moments from my past…but from a future I hadn't yet lived.

I saw Will, living in a pretty cottage with his family. Liv, sitting in a comfortable home in Boston.

And then…I saw Callum. He looked just a little older, a short beard adorning his jaw. A pained look invaded in his eyes, and I wondered for a moment if my death had done this to him.

But his expression changed to one of pure joy when a figure ran toward him.

A small girl, wearing a pretty, yellow dress.

Without question, I knew she was his daughter.

Is she my daughter too? I wondered. *Or is this destiny's way of telling me my time is over?*

The bear's paw seemed to work its way toward my face in slow motion, a distorted growl emerging from the creature's throat.

And then…as mayhem erupted, the world sped up once again.

38
INTERVENTION

Powerful explosions sounded to either side of the Throne Room as stained glass shattered, flying through the air in a storm of jagged particles.

The Ursal, distracted and frightened, spun around in search of the looming threat.

Through the shattered windows, enormous, scale-coated creatures came flying into the Throne Room, their wings spread triumphantly.

A blue dragon…and a silver one.

Dachmal and Tefyr.

I should have been relieved. Only, something about the two dragons looked…wrong.

Their eyes glowed unnaturally red, their eyes distant, unthinking, as if some outside force had taken control of them.

Merriwether was right—the dragons have been corrupted.

When I glanced up and saw who was on Dachmal's back, I finally understood. His rider was none other than Meligant, the cruel brother of the Crimson King.

Lachlan's father.

He's the one who took the dragons captive.

But when my eyes landed on Tefyr and the two figures on his back, my breath caught in my chest.

Lachlan and Lily?

Thoughts and theories spiraled through my head, and it took only a moment to realize the truth:

Lachlan had left the battle to seek help. He'd known, somehow, that this moment was coming—and he'd known Callum and I would need him.

His act of desertion had just saved my life—though I was far from certain that Meligant was the ally Callum and I wanted right now.

A sudden weight at my side drew my eyes downward to see that King Arthur's vow had come to pass. The Sword of Viviane had reappeared with the coming of the dragons.

The chamber was a sudden mess of madness.

The Ursal fled into the corridor beyond the chamber's broad doors. Lumus stared up at Meligant, who had positioned Dachmal to face him. Smoke rings rose menacingly from the dragon's nostrils, a warning to the warlock not to try anything stupid.

Lachlan and Lily leapt from Tefyr's back and dashed toward me.

"You brought...*that*...to this fight?" I cried, gesturing toward Meligant. "You know he wants the throne for himself, don't you?"

Lachlan shook his head. "Not anymore. He's...come to understand that Callum is the only true heir."

"More like Lachlan convinced him of it," Lily said, chastising Lachlan for being so modest.

I didn't particularly care about the details just now. All I wanted was to finish what we'd started.

"Come on, Sloane," Lachlan said, "let's get you healed up and finish this."

Lily was by my side a moment later, a hand pressed to my leg just below the slash marks the Ursal had inflicted. She murmured the soothing words of a healing spell and instantly, the pain subsided, the wounds sealing up.

Without waiting another moment, I shot my hand toward Callum, breaking through Lumus's spell. Callum floated to the floor and darted toward us.

"Are you all right?" he asked.

"Fine. Just shaken up."

I glanced over to the queen to see that her eyes were locked on the silent confrontation between her husband and Meligant. I could see her contemplating her next move—though she seemed too confused to make it.

"The Ursal is still out there somewhere," I cautioned, and Lily nodded. "I don't know if it will come back, but we should be wary."

"Let's hope it's clever enough to leave this forsaken place," she said.

Lachlan shifted into wolf form, crouching in wait while Meligant continued to stare Lumus down.

I could see from where I now stood that the warlock was debating whether it was a good idea to challenge the enormous dragon and his mysterious, emotionless rider.

The Usurper Queen, flustered, positioned herself behind the throne, one hand braced on its back as Tefyr took a step toward her, threatening her with a cloud of dense smoke.

With the pain in my leg entirely gone, I stepped over to Callum. "I have something for you," I told him, pulling the Sword of Viviane from its sheath. "It's time."

Callum took the weapon in hand and moved toward his sister.

"Stop!" she cried out, her fingers slipping to her ring. "Do not underestimate me! I will end you, Brother!"

"Do it, Isla!" Lumus cried as Dachmal edged closer to him. As he stared fearfully up at the blue dragon, he shifted into his large, silver wolf form, and Lachlan leapt at him, dragging him into a brawl of teeth and fangs.

When Callum ignored Isla's warning and continued to advance, she lifted both arms into the air, crying out in a language I'd never heard. The words were ugly and guttural, their meaning clear as day. The incantation sent an icy shiver along my skin, like it came from the most gruesome, cruelest magic imaginable.

A flash tore through the air, then Dachmal and Tefyr's eyes cleared for the briefest of moments before turning emerald-green.

The Usurper Queen had stolen their minds from Meligant. She had weaponized them—just as she'd wanted to do a year ago when she had first ensnared them.

The dragons quickly maneuvered around, twisting to face Lily and me as smoke rose thick and black from their muzzles. Enraged, Meligant struggled to retake control, to force Dachmal to turn back toward Lumus...but his power wasn't enough.

"They're mine!" Isla called out. "It's time to stop pretending the likes of you are any match for us."

The two full-sized dragons opened their jaws, flame crackling and brewing in their throats as Lily clung to me, terrified.

I reminded myself of what Merriwether had told me:

Do not be afraid.

"Don't worry," I told Lily. "They won't hurt us."

When Dachmal let out a warning huff of smoke, Lily asked, "Are you sure about that?"

"Not...exactly."

The truth was, I had no idea. Meligant had taken hold of Dachmal's and Tefyr's minds once already, and the poor dragons probably had no idea what was happening.

The queen had in her possession a ring that had belonged to the most powerful sorceress in history, and until it left her finger, she would hold the dragons in thrall.

Which meant there was only one way to escape our predicament.

With the Sword of Viviane in hand, Callum leapt toward his sister, who shouted a command for her mind-controlled dragons to attack.

Wincing, I thrust a conjured shield-wall in front of Lily and me, praying that it would be enough to block whatever Dachmal and Tefyr hurled at us.

Both dragons unleashed their attacks simultaneously, and Lily and I cowered behind the broad wall as fire slammed and raged against it. The heat was intense, even painful—and I knew without a shadow of a doubt that one more attack would destroy the barrier.

I didn't want to tell Lily...but if this wall failed, I didn't have the strength to summon another one.

39
THE SWORD OF VIVIANE

As Lily and I cowered, readying ourselves for a second burst of deadly flame, a blood-curdling scream tore through the air.

All of a sudden, both dragons' eyes cleared, the queen's spell broken. Dachmal and Tefyr drew their heads back, the flame dying in their throats.

As one, Lily and I turned our heads toward the dais to see that Callum was now positioned next to the throne, the Sword of Viviane in his hand.

On its silver blade was a streak of deep crimson. The Usurper Queen, on her knees before Callum, was sobbing in horror and pain.

Had he...*stabbed* her?

"There," Lily said, pointing to something at the top of the stone stairs, several feet from the queen.

The queen's hand lay on the floor, the stolen ring still on its finger.

With one swipe of the sword, Callum had sliced it off...and stolen away her ability to craft another spell. The dragons were free—and so were Lily and I.

As I stared in disbelief, the hand shrank and wilted until the stolen ring slipped off and clattered down the stairs. I sprinted and snatched it up, slipping it into my pocket.

"Do you surrender the throne, Isla?" Callum asked as he looked down at his sister. There was sadness in his voice, his eyes. But there was also a profound, otherworldly strength. The same strength I had seen in Arthur Pendragon.

Isla narrowed her eyes at him, scowling. "I will *never* surrender it to you," she hissed, her voice filled with spite. "Never! I will come for you! Lumus, too, will come for you! My servants and I will kill you and everyone you love!"

Bloodied from his fight with Lachlan's wolf, Lumus shifted, leaping over to drape an arm around her shoulders as she tucked her injured arm into her chest.

"Lumus and Isla," Callum's voice echoed, "I hereby accuse you both of treason. The penalty is death—but I am willing to be merciful, if you ask it of me."

Lumus snarled, "I will never accept your mercy, and neither will Isla! You are a pretender to the throne and nothing more!"

He launched a hand toward Callum, a terrifying spell exploding from his fingertips. Braided flame and light intermingled, tearing their way through the air.

With the Sword of Viviane clasped in both hands, Callum simply watched the spell unfurl, unafraid.

I watched as the spell collided with the silver blade, which burned with white flame, stealing away the power of Lumus's magic.

Falling to his knees, the warlock stared, wide-eyed with a fear deeper than any I had ever seen on him.

"The Sword of Viviane can only be wielded by the true king," Callum declared. "Or the true queen." Pulling his eyes to Isla, he asked, "Do you wish to hold it, Sister?"

She sneered at him.

"Once again," Callum said, "I offer you mercy."

Isla pulled herself to her feet, her bloody arm crushed against her. "Then we choose death," she said in a growl.

Callum nodded once. "Then I will take you prisoner. You will be sentenced at dawn."

"Foolish boy!" a disturbing, piercing voice echoed through the chamber. "The entire realm knows their guilt. The Otherwhere knows what sins they have committed. There must be no delay."

I had almost forgotten that Meligant was still perched on Dachmal's back, a creepy, forbidding shadow of a man.

"They must be given a fair trial," Lachlan retorted, once again in his human form. It seemed Lumus had suffered more than he had during their altercation, and for that, I was glad.

Meligant pushed back at his son.

"They *must* die," he hissed.

"Callum is king now," Lachlan replied, his tone even. "A new era is upon this land. Let's begin it properly—with justice, not murder."

Meligant smirked at him, then, leaping down from Dachmal's back, said, "As you wish, my son. As you wish."

I looked over at Callum, who looked as dumbfounded as I felt.

This all seemed too easy. The Meligant we had met in the past wasn't one to abide by anyone else's wishes. He was selfish and cruel.

What is he playing at?

"So be it," Callum said, backing away from the queen and her husband, the sword still in his hand. "Vega—would you do me the honor of shackling these two?"

I nodded, then conjured a pair of solid steel handcuffs, securing Isla's solitary hand to Lumus's.

"Try anything, and I will take all three of your remaining hands," Callum told them both.

"We wouldn't dream of it," Lumus growled.

"We will fly them to the Academy," Callum told the rest of us.

"We'll lock them in the dungeon once Isla's wound has been tended. At dawn, we'll do what we must."

He nodded toward Dachmal. "I'm sure our friends here would be happy to transport you both."

By the time I saw the dragons tighten, it was too late.

Their necks craned, their jaws opening...and then, an explosion of blue flame erupted, hurtling through the air at the two prisoners.

A scream sounded then died, and when the flames cleared, a rain of ash tumbled to the ground in feather-light, horrific flakes.

I cried out in horror and shock, leaping over to where Callum stood to bury my face in his chest.

Meligant must be behind this, I thought. He took control of the dragons again. He forced them...

I found the courage to turn toward Dachmal, and when I did, I could see that there was no trace of red in his or in Tefyr's eyes. No sign of anyone controlling their minds.

"No," I whispered. "It can't be..."

~I'm sorry, Vega Sloane, a deep, rumbling voice said inside my mind. *I have upset you.*

Without question, I knew it must be Dachmal's. He and I had been friends for a long time, and I felt him in my mind just as I had so often felt Caffall.

Why did you kill them? I asked, tears in my eyes.

~Because when we were under the queen's control, I saw the darkness of her thoughts. She is cruel, as is her husband. So often, she has hurt my fellow beasts. She has murdered so many, all for the sake of keeping her stolen throne. She did not deserve justice—and neither did her husband.

Biting my lower lip, I nodded.

He wasn't wrong.

They were the cruelest people I'd ever had the displeasure of meeting.

I didn't want it to be you, I told him, laying a hand on his neck.

~And I didn't want it to be the king, Dachmal said. *His reign should begin with joy—not with the pain of killing his only sibling. If he must punish Tefyr and me for what we've done, then so be it.*

When I pressed my face to Dachmal's neck, I felt a hand on my back. *No,* Callum's voice said. *There will be no punishment. They would have died at dawn, and we all knew it.*

Somewhere out in the Otherwhere's wild lands, Raff was now an orphan. He was alone in the world, just as so many children were…thanks to his mother.

I supposed, in its twisted way, that justice really had been served.

40
THE INFIRMARY

Two Days Later

A WARM BREEZE billowed in through the Infirmary's diaphanous white curtains, the fresh summer air sweet and soothing as it met my lungs.

My eyes landed on Merriwether, who was sitting up in his bed, a goofy smile on his lips. I understood where the expression came from when my gaze moved to Nana, who was seated on the edge of his bed, holding his hand in hers.

Despite their silver hair and lined skin, they looked like two teenagers in love, their eyes bright and hopeful.

So much had happened. We still had bodies to bury and solemn ceremonies to attend for every man, woman, Grell, Witch, and other ally who had died at the hands of the Usurper Queen's forces. Lives that had been sacrificed for moments like these, when those who had survived could find themselves at peace at last.

Our land had been reborn, though there was a great deal of work still to do.

Our land.

That was how I thought of the Otherwhere now. It was, without question, my home, and I knew now, more than ever, that I belonged here. I would live a long life roaming its roads, fields, and mountains, inhaling its wonderful air—all because fate had led us to victory.

"Ah, Vega," Merriwether called when he spotted me. "Come in and have a visit, will you?"

I stepped over, a half-smile on my lips. I was happy, of course, to see him doing so well after the injury he had sustained at the queen's hand. But a nagging worry I couldn't conceal had settled inside me ever since the moment Lumus and Isla had died.

"What's worrying you, dear?" Nana asked when I took a seat in a wooden chair by Merriwether's bed.

I snickered. "Is it that obvious?"

"I've known you all your life. So yes—it is to me."

"I think I know," Merriwether said, reaching for my hand. "You're preoccupied with thoughts of the treasure from the prophecy."

It wasn't surprising that my grandfather knew what I was thinking. After all, he knew me almost as well as Nana did.

"I still don't know what it is," I admitted. "Everything else has come to pass—Callum will take the throne tomorrow. But without the so-called treasure, the prophecy says the heir will become a tyrant. Not that I could ever imagine Callum becoming cruel, but…the fact is, he hasn't found a treasure."

The corners of Merriwether's eyes crinkled, a playful smile twitching at his lips. "Are you certain about that?"

I gawked at him, confused. "He would have told me if he'd found it," I replied. "Unless you mean it's the title of king."

"No, it's not the title." Merriwether squeezed my hand. "It's not even *you*—though I know very well that he treasures you."

"Then what—," I began, but my grandfather's smile deepened,

and he winked at me. "When he is crowned tomorrow," he said, "all will be revealed, and your mind will finally be at rest, Granddaughter."

41
CORONATION

The Next Day

DRESSED in an elegant black suit with a violet tie in tribute to Merriwether, Callum looked more handsome and kingly than ever as made his way to the dais in the Academy's Great Hall.

The chamber's stone walls, freshly polished, gleamed as sunlight tumbled through the windows to land on their smooth surface. The entire Academy seemed renewed, and the bleak, cruel magic that had cast a shadow over it in recent days had been erased in favor of beauty and joy.

Around me were hundreds of the Otherwhere's residents. Grells, Witches, Wizards, humans, Waergs, and every one of the Academy's remaining former students.

Nana sat to my left, with Merriwether by her side. Will sat on my right, with Liv next to him. When I leaned over to whisper a thanks to them for letting me drag them to the Otherwhere, Liv waved a hand at me. "Are you kidding? Do you think I would have missed this? My friend is a king! I was a matchmaker for a freaking *king*!"

She shot Will a flirtatious look, then added, "If only I could matchmake for myself…"

Will let out a chuckle. "Sorry, Liv. I'm kind of seeing someone out in California."

At that, my eyes went wide, and I elbowed him gently in the side. "Will! You didn't tell me that!"

"Her name is Diana," he said. "That's all I'm going to tell you. For now, at least."

"You should've brought her!" Liv chastised.

"Yeah, that would have been a great idea. 'Hey, I know we've only been dating for a month, but would you travel with me to a magical land to watch the coronation of my sister's fiancé who happens to be a descendant of King Arthur? It'll be fun!'"

Liv snorted. "Fair point."

I brought my eyes up to the dais again, confused.

"If Merriwether isn't crowning Callum," I whispered to Nana, "I wonder who is."

She smiled. "I suppose we'll see."

As if on cue, Callum turned to address the large crowd.

"The Otherwhere," he said, his voice deep and resonant, "is a place of exquisite beauty. A land laced with the deepest, oldest magic. To be named king is a great honor, and I do not take it lightly."

I smiled as I watched him. He was speaking as though he had always been meant to live this day—as if fate itself were compelling the words to emerge from his mouth.

As nervous as he'd been at times, it felt now like he was well and truly ready to slip into this new chapter in his life.

"But," he added.

"But?" I whispered, and I heard a chorus of similar murmurs rise in the air behind me.

"The Crimson King and the Usurper Queen have both proven over many years that the Otherwhere should not be ruled by a single individual. Power is a corrupting force—and it has not served this land well."

The murmurs grew louder. In the air, I could feel the confusion of the masses intermingle with my own bewilderment.

Callum hadn't mentioned anything to me about this. I'd assumed he would simply be crowned and that would be that.

What was he talking about?

I turned and looked at Merriwether, who was smiling slightly, as if he knew exactly what was about to occur. Had he and Callum planned this—whatever *this* was?

I sat back and inhaled deeply, trying to relax as Nana reached for my hand.

"Do you trust your Callum?" she asked in a whisper.

I nodded. "Of course."

"Then don't worry, my girl."

"You may be wondering what I'm about to say," Callum continued. "And why I am not immediately reveling in the idea that I should become a supreme monarch to reign over this realm." Callum looked over the crowd, his light eyes moving slowly from face to face as he spoke. "You see, I learned a valuable lesson some time ago. It was a person of great integrity who taught it to me—to all of us. A person who helped us to win the war." At that, his eyes landed on mine. "A person who was instrumental in bringing together the Relics of Power."

My heart leapt in my chest, my stomach churning.

What was this about?

He smiled, then pulled his gaze away and continued.

"Vega Sloane is modest. She would never wish for the praise most would heap on her for the sacrifices she has made for this land. She would never take credit for the fact that, when the time came to name her Chosen Seeker, she chose to share the title with her peers—because she knew something most ambitious leaders never come to understand. Vega knew that there is strength in numbers. And, if this brief war has taught us nothing else, it's how true that is. Without the Witches, the Grells, and all those of you who trained so hard at the Academy for so many years, we would have failed."

Callum paused for a moment before continuing. "Many lives have been lost. Great sacrifices have been made, and I take none of it lightly. For many years, the Grells of the Northern lands have been treated like second-class citizens. The Waergs have been forced to serve a cruel queen. They have been ostracized from humankind, and I don't need to tell you how wrong that is."

Callum exchanged a glance with Kohrin, who was standing to one side of the Great Hall, his eyes bright, his chin held high. Dressed in an elegant suit and tie, he looked noble and proud.

"As king, I intend," Callum continued, "to divide the Otherwhere into territories. One will be overseen by me—and that region will include my homeland of Anara as well as the Chasm in the South, which I intend to restore to its former beauty. The West will be ruled by the Witches, with Solara, Morgan le Fay's descendant, as its leader. The Mountains will be overseen and ruled by the Grells, with Kohrin Icewalker as the Warden of the Peaks. The East will be watched over by the Academy, which will still exist as a school for magic users and warriors—in case a need for their help should ever arise in the future. And last, but certainly not least, is the North."

With that, to my utter shock, Lachlan stepped onto the dais and strode toward Callum. When he was close, Callum laid a hand on his shoulder and smiled.

"My cousin—my *Brother*," he said. "Lachlan Sinclair-Drake will be Warden of the Northern Lands. There, he will welcome Grell, Waerg, and human alike. Any Waerg who was once loyal to the Usurper Queen will be forgiven, provided they agree to live peacefully among both humans and Grells."

The murmurs were no longer murmurs, but raised voices, shouting in response to Callum's words.

At first, I thought a sea of rage had begun to bubble and roil behind me. Protests from the Otherwhere's angry citizens.

But then, I heard a cry that brought a smile to my lips and a swell of pride to my heart.

"Long live King Callum!" a male voice shouted. "And long live the New Otherwhere!"

I turned around to see a wave of hands in the air, cheering Callum and the unification of the Otherwhere…

By splitting it into parts?

It made a strange sort of sense.

"Are we in an alternate universe?" I asked under my breath, and Nana laughed.

Lachlan stepped over to a table covered in a dark velvet cloth, which he pulled away to reveal a beautiful crown of silver inlaid with exquisite emeralds.

"The prophecy is fulfilled at last," Merriwether said, leaning forward. "The rightful heir has taken the throne…and he has found the treasure."

My brow furrowed. I had no idea what he meant by that, unless Callum had been on some treasure hunt I knew nothing about. "You mean the crown?"

Merriwether laughed, shaking his head. "What is the one thing Callum has always wished for above all else? What is the thing he's craved all his life?"

At those words, my eyes widened.

How could I have been so dense, so unable to see it for so long? Even the Lightsmith had known it, though he had spoken in riddles when he'd talked about it.

"A family," I breathed.

Of course. The treasure was *never* something gleaming or gold—it was never something solid. It was a feeling—one that couldn't be bought with all the gold in all the worlds.

"He's found it at last," Nana said, putting an arm around my shoulder. "You. Lachlan. Kohrin, Solara, and everyone else in this land—they're more loyal than anyone he's ever known. Callum Drake, whose parents and sister betrayed him so cruelly, has realized he can create his own family—one far stronger than those who failed him."

With tears in my eyes, I understood.

Callum stood before us with the crown on his head, his cousin Lachlan next to him, a hand on his shoulder. As they looked out at the crowd, Kohrin and Solara joined them. Together, they looked so strong, so…happy. Like every bit of pain, every struggle, every tear…had led to this moment.

"Aren't you going to join them?" I asked Merriwether. "You're the Academy's Headmaster."

But he shook his head. "It's time I retired, I think," he said, turning his head to the right to see Niala, Rourke, and Aithan the Ranger stride up and join the others on the dais.

"I thought they were moving to the North!" I said under my breath.

"I made them an offer they couldn't refuse," Merriwether said with a wink. "Niala will teach the Academy's Casters, Aithan will teach the Zerkers and the Rangers. Together, they will guide the Academy for the Blood-Born into the new era."

When all the Otherwhere's new leaders had gathered on the dais, we rose to our feet and applauded them. Will slipped an arm around my shoulders, pulling me close and whispering, "You should be up there too, you know."

I laughed. "I'm sure Callum agrees with you," I said as my eyes met the king's. "But he knows how much I hate being on a stage."

42
PLANS

After the ceremony, I made my way over to Callum, who was standing in the reception room down the corridor from the Great Hall. He had already removed his crown and run a hand through his hair, messing it up to revert briefly to the young man I had always known.

"Surprised?" he said, pulling me in for a hug.

"I am," I confessed. "But in the best possible way. You did the best possible thing for this land."

"This land deserves to survive," he replied. "And to thrive."

Callum's eyes pulled to a distant window, and I followed his gaze to see Caffall soaring through the clouds alongside Dachmal and Tefyr, who were still recovering from their ordeal.

"I never wanted to rule by instilling fear in our people," he said. "I'll need help to rebuild the towns that were burned and to repair the lands to the South. I know I have a dragon at my disposal but in the end, I'm just a man, Vega—one who happens to have descended from a powerful king."

"One who happens to have an amazing bond with that magnificent creature," I teased, watching Caffall swoop around in a serpentine pattern, playing with the other dragons as if all three of them were puppies with too much energy.

Callum turned to me to Liv and Will, who were standing some distance away. Liv appeared to be teasing Will about his new girlfriend, and I rolled my eyes and laughed.

"Have you made your decision?" Callum said, taking me by the left hand and stroking a finger over my ring. "Have you decided where you'd like to spend your future?"

I shot one more look over at Will, my throat tightening slightly. "I keep reminding myself that Will is my family," I said. "That I need to be in our world for him, for his future children. Not to mention that my parents would have wanted me to go to university and get a degree."

Callum lowered his chin and nodded solemnly. "I respect your wishes, then. I only want you to be happy. I won't try to keep you here."

"Callum!" I laughed. "You didn't even let me finish before you drew a conclusion."

I saw a flash of something in his eyes, as if a flicker of hope had just sprung to life inside him. "Finish?" he said. "But you said your parents…"

"I said my parents would have expected me to get a *degree*. And yeah, under different circumstances, Will would probably want me to have a 'normal' life. But the thing is…" I smiled up at him as I spoke. "Above all, my parents would have wanted me to be happy, and let's face it—my life *isn't* normal. I believe if my parents had known what Nana had given up to stay in our world, they would have been horrified. They loved me—and they would never have asked me to sacrifice my happiness to do what's 'normal.' Look—Will and I, we've already talked. He gave me his blessing. He has a life to live, and so do I. There's a reason I'm a Seeker, a Shadow, a Summoner. I've come to realize without a doubt that I belong in this place. The Otherwhere makes me happy. But more importantly," I said, pushing myself up onto my toes and kissing him gently, "*You* make me happy."

At that, Callum's face lit up, and once again, I saw the young man I'd first met a year ago.

"You mean..." he said.

"I mean I will stay here with you, Callum Drake," I said, tears beginning to gather in my eyes. "It was never going to be any other way."

He pulled me close, kissed the top of my head, and whispered, "I will do everything in my power to make your life beautiful."

"Don't worry," I replied. "You already do."

Pulling back, I added, "By the way—do you know what day it is in my world?"

Callum narrowed his eyes. "Is this a trick question? We both know time here doesn't correspond with time there."

"I know. But do you know what the date is in Fairhaven?"

Callum shook his head. "I'm afraid I don't. I've been a little distracted."

"Just...humor me and guess."

He looked perplexed for a minute, then slapped his forehead. "Your birthday," he said. "It's your eighteenth birthday!"

I nodded. "Liv had to remind me that I'm now officially an adult—whatever that means."

"It's about damned time you told him," Liv said from behind me. "I didn't want to say anything and rain on the king's parade, but we really should have a cake or something."

"Oh, there's a cake," said a low voice.

I spun around to see Merriwether standing a few feet away with my Nana. As I watched, he gestured to the room's far end.

An enormous, six-tiered chocolate cake appeared on an ornate wooden table, a golden crown adorning its peak.

The number eighteen was messily scrawled on one side.

"That was my idea," Liv boasted, and I burst out laughing.

Clearly, the cake was intended to celebrate the Coronation, and not my coming of age.

Typical Liv, steering the attention away from Callum.

Still, I wasn't about to turn down a slice.

As we headed over to partake, Liv grabbed me by the arm. "I never asked you," she whispered. "Was I right about the Relics? You didn't *really* need them, did you?"

I turned to her with a mock glare. "Well, let's see. The Lyre called King Arthur and his knights to battle. The Sword of Viviane, it…" I stopped, unable to bring myself to describe what the sword had actually done.

"Okay," Liv laughed. "But, like, I was right about you being super-powerful and strong, wasn't I?"

"Sure, Liv," I chuckled. "It was all about me."

"I knew it!"

Before the reception concluded, I managed to speak to Solara for a few minutes. She looked tired but strong, as if the victory had renewed her spirit and put her anger to rest at last.

Nodding over to where Lachlan and Lily were deep in conversation at the other end of the room, I said, "They're in love, you know."

Solara glanced over at them and smiled. "Oh, I know," she sighed.

I wanted to ask the inevitable question—what was going to happen if they decided they wanted to stay together—but Solara answered before I had the chance.

"The Otherwhere is a new realm now," she said. "I think it's time some of the old rules changed. Witches should be allowed to marry if they wish—without losing their status in the Covens or their powers. Lachlan saved your life—and you and Callum saved the Otherwhere. Lachlan and Lily deserve a little joy, don't you think?"

"I do," I said with a laugh. "I really do."

In the Rose Wing that evening, Callum and I found ourselves lying on the couch, my head on his chest as if nothing had changed, and as if the world hadn't gone through a momentous shift.

"You're really going to stay then," he said. "I'm not dreaming?"

"You're the king of the Otherwhere," I chuckled. "And the one thing you're concerned about is whether I plan to stay here?"

"Of course it is." He pulled my hand to his lips and kissed it. "I'm not sure I have the courage to ask this…" he said. "Even after a war, a victory, and everything else. But Vega Sloane…"

"Yes?" I asked, pulling forward and turning my head to look at him.

He stopped, his eyes locked on the ring on my finger. I glanced down to see flame dancing in the stones, which were swirling with fierce magic—but for once, the flames didn't instill fear or apprehension in my heart.

If anything, they filled me with love for the land so many of us had fought to protect.

"Will you…" Callum began, but he stopped, then swallowed.

"Callum Drake," I said, laughing, "of *course* I will marry you. Just…not yet."

Callum let out a laugh, his brows raised. "I mean, I'm not unhappy with that answer. But may I ask why?"

"Merriwether and Nana want to marry," I told him. "I don't want to take away from their special day…whenever it may be. Those two have waited way longer than us to be together, and I think we need to focus on their happiness. You and I have many, many years ahead of us."

"I couldn't agree more," Callum said. "So, let's get started. It's time to plan a wedding."

EPILOGUE

Several Years After King Callum's Coronation

CALLUM AND I DID MARRY...EVENTUALLY.

I told him I was too young, and that I was afraid Will would have a heart attack if I got married at eighteen. Naturally, he agreed to wait.

And so for a few years, we lived together, overseeing the rebuilding and restoration of what had once been the castle Uldrach.

In days past, the whole thing might have caused a scandal of sorts. But these were modern times in the Otherwhere, and people didn't worry so much about whether or not a king had officially wed the love of his life. Callum was admired and beloved, and as long as he was good to the realm, no one paid much attention to his personal life.

And so, we waited—with the promise if ever we decided to marry and have children, we would have a ceremony to celebrate our bond.

When we learned years after the War for the Throne—as it was eventually called—that I was pregnant with our first child, we finally set an official wedding date.

And so, King Callum, descendant of Arthur Pendragon, and Vega Sloane, descendant of Viviane, the Lady of the Lake, were wed on my twenty-second birthday at the rebuilt castle that we had named Dragonhaim—*Home of the Dragons*—in the fully restored town of Kaer Uther.

My brother Will also married his long-time girlfriend Diana in a beautiful ceremony out in California. As a wedding gift, I gave him my share of our inheritance—a million dollars to help his eventual family to buy a house and put some savings away for the future.

Meanwhile, Liv recently told me she was engaged to a "cute boy" (as she called him, despite the fact that he was thirty years old). His name was Malcolm, and though he may not have been a shifter or a magic user, he was just mischievous and "dreamy" enough to keep her interested and perpetually giddy.

Meanwhile, after their beautiful wedding, Merriwether and Nana made their home in a small, thatch-roofed cottage just outside of Kaer Uther.

Life in the Otherwhere was as peaceful as anyone might have expected, given its leadership and the benevolence of those who wished it restored.

I never once regretted the choice to stay in the magical realm, which never ceased to surprise me.

I heard recently that Raff had been spotted in the mountains, living among a small group of Waergs, who occasionally threatened rebellion against the king. Callum and I weren't particularly worried. After all, we had a few loyal dragons on our side—and many watchers throughout the realm.

If Raff wanted to try to rise up against us, he would have an entire kingdom to contend with.

Our life, for the most part, was quiet. For a long time, Callum and I made sure to spend at least an evening a week lounging together on the couch, telling one another stories about our past lives or making wishes for the future.

But over the years, the couch grew more and more crowded—in the best way possible. Callum and I soon found ourselves telling stories to an entirely new audience.

Our three children, named after three of the best people we knew: Olivia, Will, and Lachlan.

The End

AFTERWORD

The Seeker's series began as a sort of recollection of the days when I fell in love with books.

My love of reading began when I was about five years old—and it only grew as the years passed. When I was in grade one, I read the abridged versions of *Little Women, Black Beauty, Around the World in Eighty Days,* and *The Hound of the Baskervilles.*

I was a weird kid.

Fast forward many years, and I began to write *Seeker's World* for children and young adults. In my mind were my nieces and my nephew, and I wanted to offer up a story of escape from this world, one they could dive into with abandon. I pictured a world filled with challenges, a little romance, dragons, and other wonderful creatures.

I wrote the first five books in quick succession, and yes—I know I upset a few readers by taking so long to write the sixth.

There were many reasons for this, one of which was the loss of a few family members over the course of only a year. I lost a little of my will to hang out in the Otherwhere, which had been such a comfort to me for so long.

It was, simply put, hard to go back.

AFTERWORD

But recently, after a few emails from readers reminded me that I needed to finish, I got back on the horse I'd fallen off of—and it was a pleasure, though I didn't relish the idea of any of my beloved characters getting hurt in what was sure to be a nasty showdown.

I'd always known more or less what would happen in the end of the series, and I'm sure my readers did, too. But it was the journey, for me, that made writing these books such a pleasure. I can only hope your journey was as much fun.

Vega is a character dedicated to my nieces, but she's also very much *me* in many ways. A bit of a smartass at times, she's someone who always wants to do right, but sometimes lacks the strength and courage. She constantly looks to those wiser than her…but usually does her own thing, regardless.

I hope you've enjoyed her adventures as much as I have.

Thank you for joining us for so long, and here's to many more adventures together!

xox,
    K. A.

COMING SOON: THRALL

In the realm of Kravan, children of lower-class citizens are raised in a prison-like structure called "The Institution" from birth until

COMING SOON: THRALL

adulthood. Known as the Thralled, their powers reveal themselves around the time of their eighteenth birthday.

Every year, the Thralled who are tested and deemed harmless are chosen to leave the Institution and join the outside world as servants to the ruling class. Epics—those who are considered threats for their destructive powers—are sent away. Though none of the Thralled know for sure, they have long suspected that the Epics are killed by the Elite.

Rell has spent her entire life in the Institution, longing for the day she will be chosen to leave. She's always been certain her powers would be minimal just as her mother's were, and that she would be assigned to a life of simply servitude. However, as she nears her eighteenth birthday, she begins to fear the worst. The powers that have begun churning inside her are anything but harmless, and if the truth comes to light, she faces a grim fate at the hands of the ruling class.

When a handsome and wealthy young man visits the Institution and invites her to work in the palace's kitchens, she's ecstatic...but when a mysterious fellow worker offers her an opportunity to attend the annual Elites' Ball and to see their world for what it truly is, she begins to learn an ugly truth about the divisions between the ruling class and the Tethered.

After a life spent in near-isolation, Rell must now learn to distinguish friend from foe, and to decide if her new allies are who they claim to be...
or if they will turn out to be her greatest enemies.

Thrall is based on the fairy tale Cinderella, the first in a new Dystopian Romance series by the author of Recruitment and The Cure.

COMING SOON: THRALL

Pre-order until its release: Thrall

ALSO BY K. A. RILEY

If you're enjoying K. A. Riley's books, please consider leaving a review on Amazon or Goodreads to let your fellow book-lovers know!

DYSTOPIAN BOOKS

THE AMNESTY GAMES

Thrall | Broken | Queen

THE RESISTANCE TRILOGY

Recruitment | Render | Rebellion

THE EMERGENTS TRILOGY

Survival | Sacrifice | Synthesis

THE TRANSCENDENT TRILOGY

| Travelers | Transfigured | Terminus |

ACADEMY OF THE APOCALYPSE

Emergents Academy | Cult of the Devoted | Army of the Unsettled

THE RAVENMASTER CHRONICLES

Arise | Banished | Crusade

THE CURE CHRONICLES

The Cure | Awaken | Ascend | Fallen | Reign

VIRAL HIGH TRILOGY

Apocalypchix | Lockdown | Final Exam